Matilda Betham-Edwards

A Winter with the Swallows

Matilda Betham-Edwards

A Winter with the Swallows

ISBN/EAN: 9783337016173

Printed in Europe, USA, Canada, Australia, Japan

Cover: Foto ©Andreas Hilbeck / pixelio.de

More available books at **www.hansebooks.com**

A WINTER

WITH

THE SWALLOWS.

BY

MATILDA BETHAM EDWARDS.

LONDON:

HURST AND BLACKETT, PUBLISHERS,

SUCCESSORS TO HENRY COLBURN,

13, GREAT MARLBOROUGH STREET..

1867.

TO
MADAME BODICHON OF ALGIERS.

Fain would I link your dear and honoured name
    To some bright page of story or of song ;
    That so my praises might not do you wrong,
And I might take your thanks and feel no shame.
But be my patron, though I feebly praise
    A time, when with the swallows taking flight,
    I sought your lovely land that loves the light,
And woke anew and lived enchanted days :
Ah ! could I tell with what a glory towers
    The palm-tree flushing gold on purple skies,
    Or how white temples, each a marvel rise,
'Mid oleanders tipped with rosy flowers.
This little book were such for its own sake,
    A poet well might give — an artist take !

CONTENTS.

CHAPTER XV.

Chapter 1.

 REMEMBER wishing as a child that the " Arabian Nights " were all true; little dreaming how I should one day discover nothing to be truer than poetic fiction. For, as Browning says,—

All we have willed, or hoped, or dreamed, of good shall exist,
Not its semblance, but itself ;

and I was no sooner in Algeria than I seemed to hear story after story added to the Thousand and One, all as new, as true, and almost as wonderful.

One loses the grey and brown tints of our northern atmosphere at Marseilles ; and, after skimming the bright waves of the Mediterranean for two days, sights the coast of Libya whose story reaches from Dido down to Abd-el-Kader. The city of Algiers rises like a

B

vision from the sea, and one wants a pencil dipped in colour to give any adequate conception of it. Imagine terrace after terrace of pure white marble piled upon a sunny height with a broad blue bay below; bright green hills stretching towards a vast velvety plain on either side; beyond all, a line of snow-tipped mountains, dim and distant as clouds; and you have some shadowy idea of as fair a picture as the world can show.

Soon the lines and shadows of this picture are brought out more distinctly; one distinguishes the pretty French villas dotted about the suburban hills; the minaret of a mosque; the dome of a marabout; the tower of a lighthouse; the arches of a superb line of docks; lofty European hotels that stand between the harbour and the old Moorish town; ships at anchor in the port; gardens reaching to the shore; a palm - tree here, an olive - grove there.

The landing-place was a scene and a study that I shall never forget. The sky was of a brilliant, burning blue; and as we glided to the very foot of the glittering white quay, a hundred boats surrounded the steamer, plied by

Arabs, Negroes, Maltese, Turks, and Spaniards. In the transparent atmosphere, the dark skins and bright-coloured clothes of these stalwart fellows seemed actually to shine with a lustre, whilst the wonderful power, majesty, and grace of their wholly unfettered limbs was quite a revelation. A splendid young Arab took possession of me and my baggage, and whilst he was very likely making a sum after this fashion, —so much feminine greenness, so many francs, —I was admiring his beautiful oval face, and his perfectly proportioned limbs that seemed cast in bronze.

I arrived late in December, thus escaping the miseries or diversions (for under what circumstances cannot travellers in good health and spirits amuse themselves?) of quarantine. But a sort of lesser quarantine awaits all those foolish travellers who embark too late to have their baggage registered; and whilst other people went off in the happy assurance that their effects would be locked up and cared for, I had to wait for permission to carry my own away, or leave them to chance.

Baggage, like many another venerable thing, has got an undeservedly bad name, and most

people will pity me, though, as will be seen,
the circumstances proved bearable enough.

True, that a burning sun slanted overhead,
that ragged old Pariahs in inodorous burnouses
elbowed me to right and left, that a crowd of
dirty little Arabs and Kabyles hung to my
cloak begging for a sou ; but the comical side
of the scene outweighed all small annoy-
ances, for a fight took place over my portmanteau, as fierce as the contest of Greeks
and Trojans over the body of Patroclus.   One
after another, half-a-dozen bare-legged, brown-
skinned fellows leaped upon the spoil; and one
by one they were rebuffed by my guide Ali and
a couple of grave Moors, who seemed to have,
or rather to assume, some sort of authority.

Then ensued a series of oaths and vitupe-
rations, carried on in that *patois* Arab, so like
sneezing and jangling, and Swiss German, and
the cry of the camel, and a hundred other ano-
malies in one.   They pummelled, they stamped,
they screamed ; but on a sudden, appeared a
shabby little Frenchman, clerk of the Customs,
and all the uproar vanished as quickly as
the fisherman's giant turned himself into smoke.
The shabby little Frenchman nodded, and Ali,

like the lazy fellow he was, put the heaviest of the baggage on the shoulders of a couple of humble friends, or perhaps poor relations, and coolly walked by my side, carrying the umbrellas only.

He spoke tolerable French and talked volubly all the way. It was a beautiful country, Africa; and what numbers of English came out there,—*ma foi*, what numbers! The more the better for him; the English were so generous, and all the Arabs took kindly to them. He was a great favourite with the English himself, and if Madame wanted an honest commissionaire at any time, his name was Ali-Ben-Abdarrahman; everybody knew him on the quays.

In a quarter of an hour this honest Ali had mulcted me to the extent of several francs, and I was comfortably installed in the quiet Hôtel d'Europe, telling my friends home news, over a breakfast of roast quails, bananas, dates, and olives.

How pleasant it was to feel so far from home, and yet to find everything so home-like! French waiters brought us uncut "Ga-lignanis" and English letters just four days old. Groups of English travellers sat here and there; and we might have fancied ourselves in Paris but for the voices of Arab hawkers, crying lemons and violets in the streets, and the balmy air blown through the open windows, and the prospect they afforded us. Looking across the shipping we had a full view of the bay, whose turquoise-coloured waves just showed a creamy line where they met the shore; of the verdant hills bordering the plain of the Metidja; of the pale blue mountains beyond, and stretching like an arm round the sea, the rocky line of Cape Matifou.

But I was hurried away from these comforts and contemplations, in order that whilst my mind was in this state of waxy enthusiasm it might receive a firm Oriental impression.

Accordingly, after a moment's grace for the process of transforming oneself from a chrysalis to a butterfly,—that is to say, adapting one's clothes to a summer temperature,—I emerged into the streets. Leaving the modern French town with its open squares, its arcades, its cathedral, its museum, for another day, we entered at once into the enchanted land of the Moorish El-dje-zaïr.

It may sound very absurd, but I felt inclined to rub my eyes, and assure myself that I had not fallen asleep on my favourite "Arabian Nights," twenty years ago, and was barely awake yet! Or else, like the seed-corn found in the mummy, my old friends had suddenly come to life again in some miraculous way.

There sits Alnaschar dreaming in the sun over his basket of trumpery glass-ware; with his arms out at elbows, his grey cotton pantaloons in rags, and his shabby slippers hanging off from the heels, he looks a good-for-nothing fellow enough, and quite answering to the account of his immortal brother the barber. In a moment, he will rouse himself, kick his imaginary wife, the Vizier's daughter, and one feels tempted to wait and see the amusement of his industrious neighbour. *He* is no dreamer, that tailor, it is certain. As he sits cross-legged in his little shop, built like an oven in the wall, no machine works quicker than his nimble fingers with needle and gold thread; and if he gossips now and then, it is only to take breath. And lo! there is the shop of poor Bedreddin Hassan, the brother-in-law of Noureddin Ali and the bridegroom of the Queen

of Beauty, who, by the force of mysterious circumstances, became an alien and a pastry-cook.
He is handsome, prince-like, and melancholy,
as we imagine him ; but a pleasant smell of hot
cheese-cakes reaches the nose, those very
cheese-cakes by which he is restored to his
lignities and his bride.

A step farther, and we meet Morgiana
)ound to the apothecary's,—a well-knit, superb woman, half Negress, half Moor. What
a dignified gait she has ! What a self-posses-
sion ! What a look of resoluteness in her
handsome black eye ! She is wrapt from
head to foot in a bright blue cotton shawl,
having a single strip of crimson silk embroidery inserted across the shoulders, and in
this simple dress she has something of Greek
statuesqueness. A profusion of silver chains,
bracelets, and anklets adorns her fine limbs,
thus testifying to the liberality of the master
she serves so thoroughly.

Surely. the leader of those mischievous
young urchins must be Aladdin ! There are
half-a-score of them playing around a fountain,
all as ragged, as impish, and as dirty as can
be ; they cover you with dust, they splash

you with water, they drive you against the wall,—yet there is something in their frolicsomeness that forbids anger.

It is a comfort to think that the sinister old man watching them over the way may be the African magician, whose wonderful lamp will lead to Aladdin's wealth untold, and himself to destruction.

But I must check these fancies and come down, I was going to say, to the soberness of reality, though that is hardly the word for streets so full of colour and character as those of Algiers.

The French arcades occupy a level, lying parallel with the sea, whilst the old Moorish town is built on a steep ascent. Accordingly, no sooner do you begin climbing than you turn your back upon European civilisation, and feel to be really breathing the enchanted atmosphere of the East.

The architecture seems strange at first, but is simple enough when considered in relation to the climate. What, indeed, could be so adapted to the hot African suns as these narrow streets, through which scanty light or heat can penetrate? One wanders hither and thither, vainly trying to discover some order in the interminable network, but finds the invariable *cul-de-sac* everywhere, running straight or crooked, as the case may be, and often barely wide enough to admit two donkeys abreast. So continuous is the ascent that every street may be called a staircase, and were it not for the diversion in plenty by the way, a wearisome staircase too.

The houses are often built so closely as almost to meet overhead, and have a construction as unique as it is fanciful. Sometimes you have a line of bare white wall, only broken here and there by an iron grating or heavy door; or, finding the sky shut out on a sudden, you look up and see that the dwelling on your right communicates with that on your left by an arch; or you come upon a picturesque corner house, whose irregular sides are supported by wooden buttresses, sloping and slender, after the manner of thatch. Nothing is made to match; nothing is made to please the eye of the beholder from without; nothing is thought of but security against three enemies, namely,—the public eye, the rays of the sun, and the catastrophe of an earthquake.

We shall see by-and-by that behind these blank white walls exist dwellings as fairy-like as any described by Scheherazade, but for the present, are only concerned with the streets. These are bright and lively enough. You meet in ascending a stream of picturesque population, and at first the unaccustomed eye is positively dazzled with the scarlets, the sarffons, the greens, the purples, and the blues of its drapery as seen under a southern sky.

But one soon ceases to look through a kaleidoscope, and grows intent upon living costume and character instead.

There is a Jewess dressed as her ancestor might have been hundreds of years ago; a sallow-complexioned woman, inclined to *embonpoint*, and having the strongly-marked national physiognomy; she wears a straight, narrow skirt of rich brocade, a black silk handkerchief bound round her head, with coloured ends hanging on her shoulders, and a vest richly embroidered in gold and silver. By her side walks her pretty young daughter, wearing, in sign of her maidenhood, the most coquettish little cap imaginable, a mere teacup of gold and crimson, with a long drooping tassel.

Behind them,—is it a mummy or a ghost? —a Moorish lady shuffles along in her comical and ungainly dress of full white trousers, reaching to the ankle, and white shawl of woven silk and cotton, wrapt round her so as to form hood and mantle in one. Only her eyes are visible, but the white muslin handkerchief muffling her chin is a very unpicturesque veil, indeed. A bright sash is the only relief to this queer toilette. Close at her side follows her domestic, a jovial-looking negress, wrapt, like Morgiana, in blue drapery from head to foot, and bearing on her arm, the daintiest little baby in the world, whose tiny hands are dyed to a brilliant yellowish pink with henna.

There is a Kabyle woman fresh from the mountain fastnesses of the Djurdjura, and the so-called legitimate descendant of the old Berber race. One sees at a glance that she has neither Arab nor negro blood in her veins; the brow is square, the chin massive, the eye grey, the skin clear and red.

Her dress has a certain dignity. It consists of a long shawl-shaped piece of dyed cloth reaching to the ankles, confined round the waist with a belt, and fastened on the shoulders with metal pins. The arms and throat are bare, and are ornamented with rude chains of silver, palm-seeds, and coral. On her brow is a handkerchief fastened by a round brooch, betokening that she has borne her husband a male child.

There is something touching in the utter isolation of this wild, wandering creature, as she wanders through the friendless streets. One marvels what could have tempted her so far from her home among the mountains, and stops to ask a pitying question or two, but she shakes her head, understanding as little of French as of Arabic, and moves on.

Arabs wrapt to the chin in white burnouses, grave old Moors wearing turbans of costliest silk, Turks in brilliant suits of violet or brown merino, Biskrans from the desert, with their loose vests of gaudy patchwork, Jews in black drawers and blue stockings, Negroes — those universal dandies — in the lightest colours, of course, and having a flower stuck behind each ear, soldiers, both Spahis and Turcos — here was a spectacle brighter than any *féerie* of the Porte St. Martin. And then the shopping was so delightful! for is it to be supposed that a party of ladies can live without shopping were they transported into the desert?

Fancy row after row of little " chambers in the wall," each hung with wares, and the master working with his men behind the counter, or solemnly reading the Koran whilst waiting for customers.

These shops, or rather *ateliers*, contain all sorts of treasures, — slippers of white or pink kid, daintily embroidered with gold and silver thread, harness and trappings of rich crimson leather, mouth-pieces of amber, of coral, and of ivory, girdles of soft rainbow-coloured silks, curtains and cushions of old Arab embroidery, coffee-pots and trays of burnished metal-work looking like gold veined with coloured threads, carpets, soft, and gay, and sunny as flower-beds, lamps glittering with coloured glass and ornamented with tiny crescents, ostrich's eggs, mounted in silver and tasselled with silk, caskets and tables of mother-of-pearl, cash-meres from Tunis, pottery from Kabylia, sabres from Morocco.

But I might go on all day, and still give an imperfect list of the pretty things to be bartered for, as one walks through the old Moorish town. The Moors are something higher than artificers and lower than artists. Those who would have been excellent painters under more indulgent circumstances, become dyers, embroiderers, and *passementiers*.

It is wonderful what miracles of colour and taste come from these strange little *ateliers*. One watches the lithe brown fingers, swifter than any shuttle among threads of gold, and silver, and bright silk, wondering how such gorgeous combinations could have dawned upon the workman's mind. But the vivid scenery and brilliant atmosphere of Algeria make this plain later. The love of colour is sucked in almost with mother's milk.

We stopped every now and then to admire and ask a question or two, which, whether understood or not, was sure to be answered courteously and with a smile. There is no such thing as Arab embarrassment; and there is no such dignity as Arab dignity. I had not been a day in Algiers before this conviction dawned upon my mind.

We were about midway in the old town, when my friend stopped at a corner house having the words " *Ouvroi Mussulmane*," written over the door.

" Now you shall see a Moorish interior," she said, "and judge for yourself whether the Moors or the French show the best taste in architecture."

Having traversed a gloomy little entrance, we found ourselves in the centre of an airy court, open to the sky, with delicately carved pillars supporting the galleries; the pavements were of tiles, covered with flowers and arabesques, and in the midst was a fountain surrounded by banana-trees.

The bright blue sky overhead, the dainty white walls, the sparkle of the water, the wavy green leaves hanging over it, made a very pretty picture, but when we had ascended the staircase, we found a prettier picture still. Seated round the gallery, in rows, were about a hundred little Moorish girls, busy over embroidery-frames, their little brown legs tucked under them; their dark faces all life and merriment ; their bright clothing making them look like beds of tulips in May. A pleasant young French lady, one of the directresses of the school or workshop, came up and showed us some really superb work; soft white curtains covered with lilies and roses, cloaks of real cashmere from Tunis, worked with arabesques in white floss, scarfs fit for the Queen of Sheba, linen to please Cleopatra. How one longed to be rich, and take home such spoils for one's sober English home!

These children are alike of rich and poor parentage, and a few little Negresses may be seen among them. The only thought to spoil the enjoyment of this bright and busy scene is that, excepting in needlework, they are mostly as ignorant as it is possible to be. An effort was once made in a good direction by Madame Luce, the first originator of these Moorish schools. She began teaching her pupils to read and write, and was succeeding admirably when the veto of the Government was put upon such innovations. It seems that the Moors do not like their wives and daughters to be more learned than themselves.

Nodding farewells to the crowd of little Fatimas and Zorahs, we continued our ascent of the old city.

It seemed so strange, after all this enchantment, to dine in a French hotel off French
dishes, and hear English tourists talk of " doing
Blidah, and the desert, and Constantine." The
Barmecides' feast would have been much more
in keeping,—hungry as we were !

Chapter 2.

CHRISTMAS DAY IN AFRICA.—HOW WE KEPT HOLIDAY.—
THE HILLS AND HEDGE-ROWS.—THE ORPHANS' HOME
IN THE ATLAS.—BIBLICAL ASSOCIATIONS.—THE OLD
MAN AMONG THE RUINS.

T is Christmas Day—and what a day !
The warm blue sea hardly makes a
murmur as it flows inwards ; the sky
has not a cloud; the air is scented with violets ;
all the windows stand wide open.   The temperature is, in fact, that of a sunny, old-
fashioned May-day, and we join the stream of
happy holiday-makers bound to the country.
Carriages and omnibuses are rattling in every
direction, filled with French ladies in pretty
toilettes ; officers in their uniforms ; and poor
workmen with their families, all trim and in
tune for a day's pleasure. Who could help putting on one's best gown, pinning a flower to
one's girdle, and feeling as glad as any child?

Nothing can be more perfect than the drive
from Algiers to the suburban heights of Mus-

tapha Supérieure, whither we are bound. The
carriage winds amid verdant hills all the way.
On the one hand, you see the dome of a
Moorish palace glittering among the olive-trees,
or the white walls of a French villa peeping
from orange and lemon gardens ; on the other,
you look straight across a line of cypress-trees
to the blue bay, sprinkled with a thousand
sails, and the bluer mountains beyond. One
longed to copy the picture with jewels as
some skilful mosaicist has copied Da Vinci's
Last Supper in Vienna.

The hills are clothed with foliage on all
sides.   There is the ever-graceful olive, the
brilliant banana, the glossy palma - Christi,
the arrowy cypress, black and green like a
duck's wing, the silvery green aloe, the wild
cactus, the fan-like palmetto, the caroubier with
its grateful shade, and, lastly, though that is
rare, the palm.

The palm is the king of trees ; and only to
look at it is to breathe a wholly new atmosphere.
I don't know whether it is most beautiful when
standing alone against a bright blue sky, or
when planted in a stately alley, as in the
Jardin d'Acclimatation in Algiers. One can

never forget the grace and glory of its feathery branches, spread like wings that love the light. Only the leafless fig-trees remind you that it is winter now here ; but what is winter with a warm sun overhead and wild flowers growing everywhere ? Mignonette, rosemary, large golden marigolds, beautiful, tall asphodels sprinkle the turf, which every one tells me will be a glory of blossoms in two or three months.

An hour's drive brings us to our destination, a spacious white villa looking on Algiers and the sea. We wander with our friends through airy apartments, furnished after the Moorish style, and gather violets and roses in gardens having glorious views on either side, and then we eat an early English dinner, served by a picturesque Arab boy, dressed in white cotton trousers and violet cloth vest.

There is a home for little Protestant orphans far among these hills, and in the afternoon we drove thither, carrying bags of toys and chocolate. It was a lonely place for children to live in; a large, rambling Moorish house exposed to the winds on every side, and looking across the sea and the snow-tipped peaks of

the lesser Atlas.   No wonder the little ones
rushed to meet us joyfully, and welcomed alike
our presence and the bags of happy memory,
for our hostess was an old friend.

After having entertained us in the best
fashion they were able, showing their dog—who
might have guarded the Hesperides, he was
so fierce,—their school-room and their books,
they took us into the playground and sung
hymns.

The singing of orphan children is touching
at all times, but it was inexpressibly so as we
heard it here.   These little girls were mostly
Alsatians or Germans, and utterly cut off from
family love and life.   As they sung their simple
hymns among the wild African hills, one felt
comforted by the thought that the grave has
no cares, and that the poor mothers of these
children knew nothing of their isolation.   They
looked happy and healthy however, and are
well fitted by early training to become colonists'
wives, their probable destiny.

In the country it is not so much the Arabian Nights, as the Bible and the Koran, of
which you are reminded.   Hundreds of texts
that brought little or no meaning as I heard

them Sunday after Sunday in my childhood
became suddenly new, and true, and beautiful,
thus illustrated. The most trifling incident
recalls some beautiful pastoral. The most
simple feature in a landscape strengthens some
familiar, though hitherto imperfect simile. One
interprets Biblical and Mahometan history by
the aid of commentaries wholly new; and as I
drove among the olive-clad hills, I. was realiz-
ing much that had hitherto been myth only.
Jacob falling on the neck of Esau and kissing
him; the company of Ishmaelites seen by
Joseph's brothers with their camels bearing
spicery, and balm, and myrrh; the son of Kish
seeking the asses that were lost; David keeping
his father's flocks on the hills,—all these pictures
were photographed in my mind's eye from life.
It is indeed almost impossible to estimate the
beauty of such pastorals and the imagery of
such poetry without their help.

Who can understand "the shadow of a
great rock in a thirsty land," till he has
suffered the heat and blessed the shadow? or
how beautiful the spring can be in the south,
"when the rain is past and gone, the voice of
the turtle is heard in the land, and the fig-tree

putteth forth her tender leaves ;" or how much
real glory and wealth are suggested by " the
dromedaries of Midian and Epha, the multitude of camels and the flocks of Kedar," unless
he knows something of the primitive and pastoral life of the East ?

We met troops of Arabs, some mounted on
camels, others riding little donkeys side-saddle
fashion, driving a flock before them, laden with
oranges and poultry; now and then a stately
Cadi sitting bolt upright in a saddle that Sinbad
might have embroidered.

And we saw two lovely pictures.   The first
was by the wayside—a man guiding a donkey
on which were seated his wife and child.   He
strode on before us; and in the level light of
sunset, the little group looked so distinct, and
yet so dreamy, as not to belong to our world
at all.   The man was a superb creature, wild,
bearded, with marvellously symmetrical features,
and he carried his rags as if he had been a king
clothed in purple.   The woman was decently
dressed in white, and bent her veiled face over
the child, who had a bunch of freshly plucked
oranges in its little hands and crowed with
joy.

We had hardly lost sight of them when we alighted to take coffee in a little café, hidden in a perfect thicket of wild cactus and aloe. Two or three Arabs sipped coffee and chatted, reclining on stone benches after the stately Roman fashion, and nothing could equal the grace of their salutation and the perfect subjection of their inquisitiveness to good manners. They were well dressed, and spoke tolerable French, thus implying a certain European culture; but just behind this little scene of care and enjoyment, was such a suggestion of ruin and desolation as could not be forgotten.

At the back of the café were the ruins of a Moorish house, a column here, an arch there, a fragment of coloured pavement telling of former magnificence. The windows were overgrown with palmetto, and the basin of the fountain was dry, whilst what had once been the court was choked with stones and weeds.

A little donkey browsed about the court; and sitting under a broken arch, was an old man, so motionless and picturesque as to look a part of the picture, and not a living being like ourselves. His beard was white, his face pale and melancholy, his eyes lustrous; and as he sat thus, wrapt in white from head to foot, and no more heeding our presence than if we had been a swarm of mosquitoes, it was impossible not to imagine some romantic story about him.

Had he come there in the sunset to imagine a vision of prosperity now past away? Did he see "a stately pleasure dome" where we beheld ruin and desolation only? Did he mistake the wind that whistled through the loopholes, and our Frankish talk, for gay music and familiar voices long since hushed?

When, a little later, we looked back from the path by which we had come, he was still in his old position. I feel as if I should find him sitting amongst the ruins a hundred years hence could I live to see!

Chapter 3.

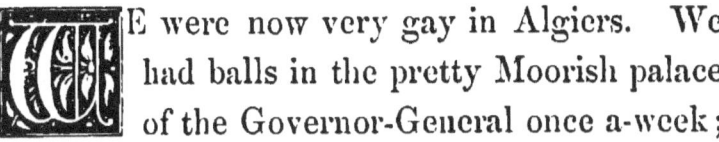E were now very gay in Algiers. We had balls in the pretty Moorish palace of the Governor-General once a-week; the Theatre was open every other night; a band played in the public square from four to five o'clock daily; every packet brought news and travellers, and the weather was so fine and warm that we could make excursions without fear.

During the first weeks of the year I led the pleasantest life; in the morning, studying Arabic, trying, oh, so hard! to master the pronunciation of that terrible twenty-first letter *Gain*, on which learned Germans have written volumes; in the afternoon, wandering about the streets, picking up such waifs and strays of Oriental life as offer themselves, and, in the afternoon, driving among the fertile and fragrant hills that encircle Algiers.

Last night we went to what is simply called an *Aïssaoua Fête;* and as, I daresay, this name suggests no more horror to you than it did to me, I will give it without explanation, that you may have the full benefit of a surprise.

Legends are not interesting except at a peculiarly poetic turn, or I would give you the history of *Aïssaoua,* that poor and pious Mahometan saint, who, in the desert, commanded his hungry followers to eat scorpions, and they would be nourished; cactus-leaves, and they would receive no harm; burning coals, and their faith would be rewarded.

We were a party of ten in all, and having dined merrily at the hotel, climbed the old tower under conduct of an Arab.

It was a superb night. The sky had not a cloud. The moon shone with wonderful brilliance. As we followed our guide through street after street, so narrow as to admit of only three or four people passing at a time, the light and shadow played fantastic tricks on every side. It was difficult to believe that shadow could be so real; still more difficult to believe that light could be so shadowy. Sometimes we passed a round archway under which lay a sleeping figure, rather two sleeping figures, one of a man, the other of his second and stranger self.

Sometimes we looked up at the white radiance of the terraced roofs, doubting whether they could be other than visions, so marble-like and unreal did they look against the glowing purplish black heavens.

As we came upon a couple of Moors talking in a doorway, every line of their white drapery was sharpened in the marvellous light as if cut out of marble, themselves more shadowy than any shadow, looking, in fine, like statues, and not in any degree human beings with ourselves.

We had climbed for upwards of half-an-hour, when our guide entered a mole-track of a street, and stopped at a house, the very walls of which seemed beating and bursting with barbarous music. It was so dark and the music was so infernal, that I think if it had not been for the protection of three or four gentlemen, the ladies would have lost courage and run away. I felt a terrible coward, but dared not own it. Following our guide, we now pressed pell-mell into an open doorway and groped our way within, elbowed and jostled by a crowd of Arabs, thin, ragged, clean or dirty, as the case might be. Once inside we found everything bright, and cheerful, and gala-like. The court was spacious and spread with bright-coloured carpets; lights were abundant, chairs were placed for the better order of spectators in a semi-circle, and the action of the play had not yet begun.

Opposite to us stood about fifty men in a circle, their clothes for the most part of brilliant colours, their dark faces rapt and eager, their voices mingling in a prayer, of which the name " Aïssaoua, Aïssaoua," and the formula, " La-allah-illa-allah!" " There is no God but one God!" formed the burden. Behind them squatted three or four musicians looking demons of sound from drum, castagnettes, and tambour; whilst the doorway through which we had come, grew every moment more crowded with spectators,— Jews, Turks, and Arabs, mostly of somewhat disreputable appearance. Only one or two French soldiers kept us company.

By-and-by coffee was prepared in a little

kitchen close behind us with an officiousness of hospitality delightful to witness.

How could people prophesy such horrors to us? According to all authorities, learned as well as familiar, an Aïssaoua fête was everything that was ghoul-like, revolting, and unearthly; whereas we were treated to some excellent coffee, a picturesque assemblage, and some extraordinary moonlight effects. But when coffee had been served, a new spirit began to animate the musicians, and for about an hour they subjected us to a torture impossible to describe. Our teeth were slowly drawn one by one, our tympana were beaten and bruised, our flesh was pricked with infinitesimal pins, our nerves were twisted and strained almost beyond endurance.

In the midst of this absurd suffering, which we only bore because we hoped for a reward afterwards, came a shrill, long-continued cry. It was such a cry as some antediluvian monster like the Plesiosaurus might have given when swooping on its prey, and I looked right and left wondering in vain what throat could have uttered it. Again and again it sounded above drum and tambour, the unearthliest, cruellest,

most horrible applause I ever heard in my
life; and at last I discovered from whence it
came.

The court in which we were seated was
open, and ranged in rows around the uppermost
gallery, were some dozen women, their white
immovable figures looking like ghosts against
the background of the dark purple sky, their
muffled faces bent eagerly over the balustrade.
The voices of the women seemed to act like
poison on the brain of both musicians and
Aïssaoua. The tambours evoked sounds more
diabolical still, the chants became more frantic.
At last the spell worked, and one of the men
broke from the ring and began to dance.

And what a dance! One was reminded
of Goethe's ballad and the skeleton that performed such weird feats on the moonlit graves,
and of everything fiendish or fantastic that the
imagination of man has conceived.

The body was bent backwards and for-
wards, the head was shaken, the breast was
struck with a frenzied agility and recklessness,
till the performer looked as unlike anything
human as could possibly be. Now his head,
with its horrible mass of snaky hair, hung

backward as if dislocated; now his breast resounded with such blows that you feared some
blood-vessel were broken; now he whirled to
and fro, yelling, raging, glaring.

Soon another and another Aïssaoua were
seized with the spirit, and now the sight became
horrible. They caught hold of each other by
the waist, swaying this way and that, foaming
at the mouth, wriggling like snakes, howling
like hungry wolves, and never breaking the
frightful Mezentian union, till one by one each
fell upon the ground either in a tetanic swoon
or a cataleptic convulsion. To see these revolting figures writhing at our very feet, to
hear the shrill choruses of the women and the
monotonous txchs-t-t-t-r-r-r-mmm — txchs-b-b-b-
m-m-m of the musicians, was enough to drive
away the most inquisitive ladies in the world,
but our failing courage was filliped by such
whispers as these: " What a scene for you—a
painter, or for you—an author!" " You are
English ladies, and own to cowardice ?" Or,
" Oh! they are only charlatans, and do it to
gain *soldi.*" Or, " The grand *coup-de-bataille*
is yet to come. We have seen really nothing
as yet."

So we stayed, not without dreading, if this were done in the green tree, what would be done in the dry ; and some furtive glances at the little cave of a kitchen behind us, where all sorts of diabolical preparations were going on. There was a little fire-place in one corner, and the Arab who had prepared our coffee knelt before it, heating flat pokers among the red-hot embers, whilst a big blue-black negro busied himself complacently among fragments of glass, knives, scorpions, needles, swords, and broad leaves of the prickly cactus.

Meantime, the Aïssaoua recovered from their swoons and staggered hither and thither, contorting themselves in the most wonderful manner, foaming at the mouth, looking as the evil spirits might have looked when driven out of the swine. And now the instruments of torture were exhibited, the exulting cry of the women rose to a higher pitch, the Mussulman crowd became ungovernably enthusiastic, and the Aïssaoua were fired with the spirit of faith.

The scene now grew infernal. The Mo-kaddem, or Aïssaoua priest, held out a leaf of the Barbary fig, bristling with thorns an inch in length, and his disciples knelt round him, snapping, biting, tearing the horrid food like ravening beasts. Then a basket of blazing coals was brought out, and they fell upon them greedily, rubbing them between their hands, making a carpet of them to dance on, grinding them between their teeth. One terrible-looking creature, a negro, walked about the court holding in his mouth a red-hot cinder, and looking like nothing so much as the Devil of primitive imagination. Then he dropped it on the ground with a fiendish cry, "Aïssaoua, Aïssaoua," and grovelled over the glowing fragments, picking up one at a time with his teeth.

But the worst was yet to come; for now red-hot irons were brought from the fire, with which they proceeded to seethe and scorch themselves in a manner perfectly sickening. They applied them gently, as one applies a plaster, to the soles of their feet, the palm of their hands, the flat part of their arms; and all this was done with an ecstatic delirium that went far to overthrow the suspicion of charlatanry.

The smell of burning flesh, the howls, the

groans, the contortions of the Aïssaoua, the universal madness, now became unendurable. The men of our party jested no more, but looked on as horrified as ourselves ; we ladies huddled together, shrinking from the wild figures yelling about us, and only longing to get away.

As soon as exit became possible we made way to the door, having sufficiently supped on horrors for one night.

How delightful to breathe the fresh air of the night again, and leave such a world of fantastic devilry behind ! On our way home we naturally discussed the claims of the Aïssaoua to true fanaticism. A., who was like myself a neophyte in Algerian experiences, and an artist, declared the whole affair to be a bit of barbaric enthusiasm, *pur et simple*. B. and C., who were gay young German doctors, argued on the same side, averring that as far as their experiences went, no Revivalism was ever more sincere ; adding, "They couldn't deceive us as to the fainting fit and the bleeding mouths, you know." D., a French painter, and a sceptic, said that it was a parcel of trickery from first to last, though, as his little wife observed sagely, he had been the first to run away. F., who was an Algerian by virtue of many years' residence, said that it was half quackery and half religion, and that a year or two back she had seen a live donkey torn to pieces by these very Aïssaoua. G., a very practical person, clenched the argument against them, saying slily, "They seemed glad enough to collect francs from us, which looked very much as if they made a trade of tormenting themselves." And this was true, for on our entrance we had all been more or less mulcted. We found ourselves at the hotel without having reached any unanimous conclusion excepting one,—namely, to go to no more Aïssaoua fêtes.

But I am glad to have seen one. My storehouse of African recollections is so bright that I can afford to have the skeleton of a horror in the background.

Chapter 4.

AN ARAB'S OPINION UPON ALGERIAN AFFAIRS.—THE CHEAP-
NESS OF LIVING AT BLIDAH.—ARAB AND NUMIDIAN
HORSE.—MAHOMETAN LEGENDS.

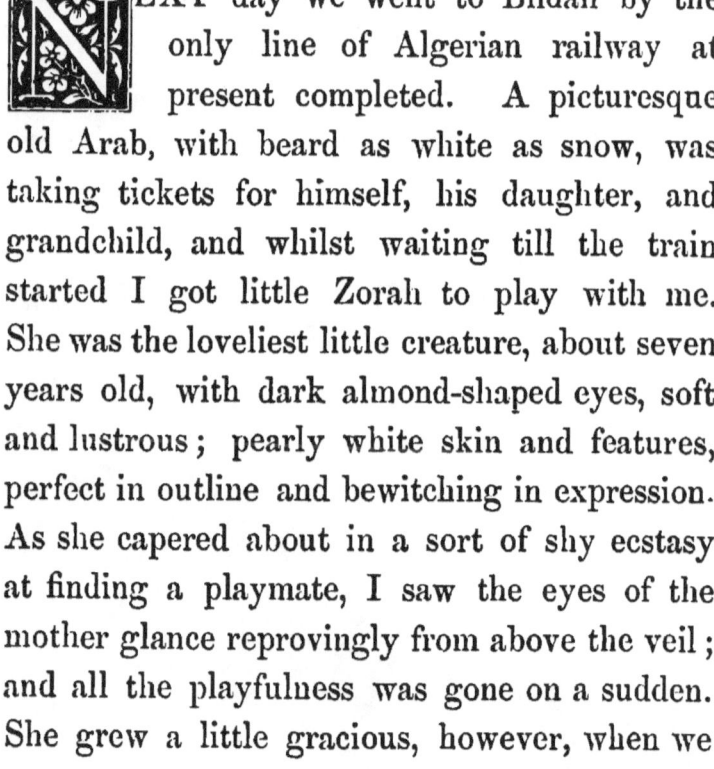

EXT day we went to Blidah by the only line of Algerian railway at present completed. A picturesque old Arab, with beard as white as snow, was taking tickets for himself, his daughter, and grandchild, and whilst waiting till the train started I got little Zorah to play with me. She was the loveliest little creature, about seven years old, with dark almond-shaped eyes, soft and lustrous; pearly white skin and features, perfect in outline and bewitching in expression. As she capered about in a sort of shy ecstasy at finding a playmate, I saw the eyes of the mother glance reprovingly from above the veil; and all the playfulness was gone on a sudden. She grew a little gracious, however, when we praised the child's beauty pantomimically, and we talked together as well as we could. She said that her father was a marabout (descendant of a saint), which very likely accounted for the respect shown to him. These marabouts are a plentiful aristocracy; we encountered marabouts or tombs of marabouts everywhere. The patent of their nobility is the legend of a miracle-working ancestor.

After traversing the plain of the Metidja, and the fertile French villages of Boufarik and Bintuta, you come in sight of Blidah lying like a white dove in a nest of green. It is a pretty little town, stretching terrace-wise at the foot of the Lesser Atlas, and belted with orange groves. No wonder that it has been fancifully called the Garden of the Hesperides. Whichever way we went, we were sure to find ourselves in such gardens as the heart of Mignon longed for:—

> " Wo die Citronen blühn
> Im dunklen Laub die Gold-orangen glühn,"

and to the unaccustomed eye, the mass and depth of colour were at first dazzling. For the first day or two of our stay we lived entirely in these gardens, many of them still kept by a dog as intractable as the dragon Ladon.

After the glare and heat and glitter of the Algerian streets, there was something inexpressibly refreshing in the quietude of the dusky orange and lemon groves. Looking upward we seemed to breathe under a firmament wholly new,—a firmament of lustrous green, lit by stars of more than golden splendour. Not a sound, not a glimpse of the outer world penetrated these solitudes ; before, behind,—to right, to left, stretched gardens as gorgeous as those Aladdin discovered by aid of the Lamp, and to us as enchanted.

There were oranges of all sizes, constellations of the Great Bear, the Pleiades, and the Milky Way ; whilst here and there a bough covered with blossoms perfumed the air, as only orange-blossoms can. Then there were groups of the lemon-tree, with its leaves of pale transparent green and primrose-coloured fruit, and lines of stately cypress hedging in and protecting all this beauty and wealth like sentinels. It was delightful to be idle in such a

scene, whether the unseen sun shone overhead,
or a tender rain pattered on the glossy leaves
and brought down golden spoils to our feet.

For one of the so-called winter rains came on,
and compelled us to seek diversion near home.
There was plenty at hand. In the first place,
we made the acquaintance of a very intelligent
proprietor of orangeries, who gave us his story,
including the history of the Algerian orange-
trade during the last few years. We heard it
in the large store-house attached to his gardens,
where a negro and a couple of French women
were busily sorting oranges and lemons.
Piles of the brilliant fruit dazzled the eye on
every side. The ground was heaped with it;
the walls were hidden by it; the air was
perfumed with it. In spite of this plenty, it
seemed startling to be told that the grower
had to part with his oranges for three-halfpence
a hundred.

Whilst talking trade and statistics, I was
looking all the while at the busy negro opposite
to me. If any one could look blacker than
a negro he did then, as his figure stood out like
a bas-relief in jet against the back-ground of
warm gold and amber.

Having learned all that we wanted to know about oranges, and gained the impression that it would be a very profitable as well as poetic thing, to hire a corner in the Garden of the Hesperides, we strolled through the town. Such a dull little French town it was! in spite of the beautiful hills stretching above and around, and the prettiness of its aspect as seen from the plain.

There was a gateway at each end, and a square in the midst, and a little church and a big barracks; and hundreds of majestic Arabs and trim little French soldiers wandering about, not knowing in the least what to do; and one or two real Arab streets, with quaint little mosques and marabouts,* and deliciously cool cafés full of stately coffee-drinkers, in such attitudes as to drive a sculptor wild.

We went to one of these cafés and drank coffee, partly because we were cold, and partly because we wanted amusement. There were only two or three men there, a richly dressed Caïd, a couple of ragged but stalwart Kabyles, and an intelligent and gentlemanly Arab merchant of Blidah, who spoke French exceedingly

---

* The consecrated tomb of a Mahometan saint.

well. Coming as we do, full of prejudice against the Mahometan theories concerning women, it is impossible not to be struck by the deferential behaviour of Arabs to all those European ladies with whom they come in contact. In this café, for instance, ladies could but be in the way, yet an honourable place was yielded to us, and every respect was paid to our comfort in a manner quite touching to witness.

It may be urged that the Arab is too much of a Jew not to know how greatly the annual influx of rich English visitors adds to his profits; but every Arab is not a merchant, and, moreover, what so easy as to distinguish between selfish servility and disinterested good-nature?

One of our party, a practical inquisitive Swiss *propriétaire,* put some rather downright questions to the friendly merchant, who did the honours of the café. "Tell me," he said; "do things go better or worse with you than they did with your father and grandfather when the Turks were strongest in the land?"

"Oh, monsieur, what a difficult question!"

"You can speak freely. We are all friendly people. I am Swiss, my wife is German, those ladies are English — to whom should you talk confidence if not to us ?"

"I tell you frankly then that we are worse off."

"But why? Money is brought into the country. Roads are made for you. Railways are laid down for. You are helped instead of hindered."

"Ah, no, monsieur; don't you see that men cannot use new tools at once? The French are too quick for us. They get before us. It is they who are helped, and we who are hindered."

"But you Arabs must quicken your pace and overtake them. You must struggle with them on equal grounds. You must use their roads, their steam, and their ships. You must out-buy them and out-sell them in the markets; or they will beat you in the race."

"Without doubt they will beat us."

"Is it not your own fault? In coming here I saw some farms so fertile as to remind me of my native Switzerland. They belonged to French colonists. I saw here a silk-mill, there a cotton-factory. They were carried on by French enterprise. Who gets the best harvest? The Frenchman with his iron ploughs and harrows, not the Arab with the lumbering bits of wood he calls 'tools.' I tell you, monsieur, you have only to use your money and your wit to outstrip the colonists."

Whereupon the merchant shook his head, and said that very few Arabs had much money now-a-days, and that fewer still had the enterprise to risk it.

"There we have you again," continued the Swiss, "how can such sensible fellows as you Arabs bury your money in a hole, and never make more of it from year to year? The inconceivable notion! You must do away with these outlandish practices, and all will go well."

"That will not be in my time," answered the merchant resignedly, and then the subject was dropped.

It is quite true, though hardly to be believed, that the Arabs do bury their money in the ground ; and it is also true that very few of them have much to bury.

But whilst the richest set such an example of uncompromising conservatism, how can anything like enterprise be expected of the poor? Many Algerians hold a theory that the Arab, like the American Indian, will become an

extinct race. From all that I have read and
seen, I am unable and unwilling to believe it.
Taking the Blidah merchant as a fair type of
his class, I should say that the only influence
wanted to raise him on a level with the con-
quering race, is that of free and extensive
foreign intercourse. This seems the more
practical, since many civil appointments are
open to the natives, and the boys of the better
class are all taught French.

We stayed several days at Blidah, and
arrived at some statistical information which
may interest all ladies who do not keep housekeepers. People can live upon absolutely
nothing in the Garden of the Hesperides.
After having inquired the prices of provisions
and the rent of houses, I should indeed be
sorry to affirm how far two hundred a-year
would not go. Everything is plentiful, the
woods are filled with game, the land runs over
with milk and honey, oranges are to be had six
for a half-penny,—or indeed for the asking,—
and the banks are covered with wild strawberries.

Those who have a very small fortune and
a very large family should come to Blidah—

always supposing them not to be afraid of
earthquakes. They would find a land of
Goshen, and a lovely land too ; a climate as
nearly approaching perfection as I suppose
any climate can be ; schools alike for boys
and girls, and that best of all educations,
namely, the untrammelled life of a primitive
society.

I never saw a group of rosy-cheeked children playing about some neat little homestead,
without contrasting their present home with the
one they had probably left,—in Paris, Alsatia,
or the most crowded cities of Germany. Some
of the villages around Blidah were depopulated
again and again by marsh-fever, but by dint of
indefatigable drainage have been turned into
such little oases of cultivation as would almost
satisfy a Suffolk farmer ; for what Sidney
Smith said of the Australian soil may be
applied to the Algerian, "But tickle it with
a hoe, and it will laugh into a harvest." Anything and everything can be done with it; and
though French colonization in Africa is not a
strong point in the national vanity, I see no
reason for the general hopelessness expressed
regarding it. Americans say to you, "How

can a country prosper with no rivers?" Colonists say, "What can we do whilst the Arabs burn our crops and forests?" The English say, "Oh, the French will never succeed in Algeria, because they only come in the hope of making money and returning home. They should settle down as we do in our colonies.".

But though it is substantially true that the want of rivers, the Arab incendiaries, and the character of the colonists themselves, war against Algerian prosperity, it is also true that there are remedies at hand. With good railways and roads, with a more discriminative treatment of the Arabs, with a better class of colonists, what could not be done with such glorious crops of corn, of olives, of tobacco, and of cotton ?

Of course, the greater number of the contributors to that extensive "Bibliothèque Algérienne," which has cropped up within the last few years, propose a hundred and one revolutions, generally of a tendency decidedly anti-Arab. I have read dozens of these books, and have always come to the conclusion that the book is yet to be written which shall do justice alike to the native and the colonist. Without being *un Arabophile*, and without overlooking a single fault of the Arab, it is impossible not to feel a little sympathy with him. It is undoubtedly true that his theory regarding women militates against any great advance in social and intellectual elevation; but in what way do his religious or social theories hinder him from becoming a useful member of society and a participator in government?

And, speaking from an artist's point of view, what a loss it would be to the lovers of the picturesque, if every stately Caïd donned the European paletôt and hat, and every lovely Moorish house gave place to an ugly French villa? Every day the world grows more uniform, and I dare say these things will come sooner or later; but if the Arab would mix sufficiently with the European to content himself with one wife, and grant her a more intelligent life in this world and the next, I think the most enthusiastic innovator would be content.

There is a very romantic and picturesque gorge near Blidah, where you see apes jumping about on the trees in fine weather, and ferny banks rivalling those of Devon or Cornwall. A more isolated part cannot be conceived, and yet, though we visited it on a wet day, we found a couple of Englishmen driving in its most solitary part!

On the way thither you see wretched Arab villages, mere piggeries of wood and mud, with fine well-grown children playing about as happy as princes.

What delighted us at Blidah, next to the orange-groves and the farms, was the sight of about fifty horses belonging to a regiment stationed there. A belief in Arab horses comes as naturally as a belief in " Paul and Virginia;" and all the old childish enthusiasm returns as soon as one sees these superb little creatures in their native country. One grows a little puzzled as to the proper demarcations between the Persian, Numidian, Syrian, and pure Arab races; but General Daumas assures us that the terms are all synonymous, and mean the Oriental horse exclusively. All lovers of horses should read his book about them, which abounds in fact and fancy, and is as diverting as a sensational novel from beginning to end.

The Mahometan legends regarding the horse are poetic in the highest degree. When the Lord wished to create the horse he cried to the south wind, "I would fain have a creature born of thee; condense thyself." Then came the angel Gabriel, and took a handful of the condensed wind, and presented it to the Lord, who made therefrom a light bay horse.

The horse prays three times a-day.

In the morning he says, "O Allah, make me dear to my master!"

At mid-day, "Be good, O Allah, to my master, that he may be good to me!"

And at night, "May my master, O Allah, win Paradise on my back!"

One day the Prophet was asked by one of his followers if there were horses in Paradise.

"If God permits you to enter Paradise," he said, "you will have a horse of ruby furnished with wings, by which he will bear you whither you will." His own horse Bourak went there. And an Arab poet has sung:—

· "Who will weep for me after my death? My sword, my land, and my beautiful bay of the slender form."

One could fill pages illustrative of the traditionary love of the horse, which has been handed down from generation to generation, and the subject is so bewitching that one is tempted to do so. But I will content myself with dipping here and there into General Daumas' book, recommending the enthusiastic reader to such collections of Arab poetry and legend as lie within reach.

In the Sahara the horse is reared as tenderly as the heir-apparent to a throne. When the foal is weaned, the women say, " This orphan belongs to us ; let us make his life as easy as possible." The diet and training are attended to with the utmost care and regularity. Amulets and talismans are hung round his neck to preserve him from wounds, sickness, and the evil eye. The women and the children are his playfellows. He is fed with date, kouskous, and camel's milk. In times of famine his master will stint wife and child that his horse may not suffer.

" Every grain of barley," says the Prophet, " given to your horse shall bring you a pardon in the other world."

And a sage has said,—

" The noble may labour with his hands

under three circumstances without blushing: namely for his horse, his father, and his guest."

And another,—

"Never strike a noble horse, for that is but to brutify him, and drive his pride to resist your authority. Words and signs are sufficient wherewith to correct him."

"A thorough-bred," says Abd-el-Kader, "a real drinker of air, should have long ears, long head and neck, long fore-limbs, short hind-quarters and back, large forehead-chest, large chest, clean skin, eyes, and hoofs."

The horse of the Sahara, in fact, should have all the desirable qualities of other animals, such as the courage of the bull, the swiftness and far sight of the ostrich, the endurance of the camel, and so on. The seller of such a treasure will say,—

"It is not my horse that I offer, but my son. He has such sight that he can see a hair in the night.

"He can overtake the gazelle.

"When he hears the voices of the maidens he cries with joy.

"When he finds himself on the field of battle, he rejoices in the hissing of the balls.

" He understands as well as a son of Adam; only speech is wanting to him.

"He is so light that he could dance on the bosom of your mistress without causing her to tremble.

"He has no brother in this world; he is a swallow."

Anecdotes and legends bearing upon the pricelessness of these beautiful creatures abound. One day an Arab was sending his son to market to buy a horse. Before setting out, the young man demanded what kind it was to be. The father replied, "His ears should always be moving, turning now this way, now that, as if he heard something; his eyes should be restless and wild, as if he were intent upon something; his limbs should be well proportioned and well set."

" Such a horse," said the son, "will never be sold by his master."

But I must come back to sober reality and the fifty horses of Blidah, which are no longer fed on dates and kous-kous, and sleep under their masters' tents in the desert, but belong to French officers. Indeed, it is not the Arab and his horse that present themselves before you in Algeria as inseparable ideas, but the Arab and his donkey, and, I am sorry to say, often a very scrubby, ill-used donkey, too.

Doubtless, in the desert, the old tradition and the old love remain as strong as ever, though it is hard to believe so. Excepting an occasional Caïd mounted on a frisky little Barb, one sees nothing but camels, mules, and donkeys, the two former in tolerably good condition, the latter starved, uncared for, and often bleeding from repeated blows. It makes one sick to see all the sore hides and patient faces of these poor little animals, that spoiled so many a beautiful Algerian landscape to my eyes. I am thankful to say that some high-spirited and humane ladies have got up a Society for the Prevention of Cruelty to Animals, which must, in some degree, hinder much un-necessary and shocking cruelty.

Chapter 5.

A TRIP INTO KABYLIA—FRENCH ENTHUSIASM ABOUT THE
KABYLES—LOVELY ASPECT OF THE VILLAGES—A FRENCH
SETTLEMENT IN THE HEART OF KABYLIA—SPLENDID
SCENERY—POTTERY.

HE Kabyle, or Berber, is the pet of
the French community in Algeria.
Whenever you hear an intelligent
politician discussing the relative qualities of
Arab and Kabyle, you are reminded of some
stern schoolmaster awarding whacks to the
bad boy, and cakes to the good.

This enthusiasm is not confined to politi-
cians and their press.   All Algerians are bitten
with the same fever, and even tourists and
valetudinarian visitors fall a prey to it.   I have
discussed the matter with all sorts of people
well able to give an opinion,—French colonists,
Jesuit priests, Trappist brethren, and no matter with whom, I was sure to get much such
an apology as this :—

" There is no comparison between the Arab

and Kabyle.   The Kabyle builds houses, plants
trees, tills the ground, and is a monogamist.
The Kabyle woman is really a woman, and
not a piece of furniture, or a beast of burden,
as with the Arab.   The Kabyle is a first-rate
soldier, as we have proved in the Crimea, in
Italy, in Senegal, and in Mexico.   In a hundred
years the Kabyle will be a Frenchman."

I have purchased and read a dozen books
treating of Arab and Kabyle, and found every
author a philo-Kabyle too.   Here and there,
one meets with somebody inclined to do justice
to the Arab, but it is generally the Kabyle
who gets all the pudding.   A stranger setting
foot for the first time on Algerian soil accepts
these conclusions unwillingly.   It is not, however, so easy to forget that splendid comet of
Arab civilization which has left such a trail of
light behind it.   For, as Ernest Renan has said,
" We may, without exaggeration, attribute to
the Arab half of the intellectual work of
humanity;" and whatever the present condition of his race may be, a very slight consideration of the past is a prejudice in his favour.
Setting the glories of Arab architecture and
the enchantments of Arab poetry against the less

poetic but solid Berber virtues of stability and thriftiness, the former naturally touch the beam.

But now I will describe the Kabyles and Kabylia exactly as I saw them, leaving the reader to form his own opinion.

At six o'clock, on a bright March morning, our horses' heads were turned towards the plain, and we set out, with the pleasant feeling that to-morrow would find us in a wholly new world.

There is something grand, and, at the same time, lovely, about this plain of the Metidja, which lies between Algiers and the Atlas Mountains. Lights and shadows fall about it, white villages glisten here and there, the turf is like a gaudy carpet with wild flowers, and the length and breadth of it seem interminable. Even when Algiers looks like a white line in the distance our journey is but half over.

Our driver, a waggish Maltese, managed his horses well, and by five o'clock we were at our halting-place of Tiziozou. Early next morning we were again on the road with fresh horses, and the prospect of reaching our destination in a few hours.

Soon after leaving Tiziozou, we crossed a

broad river-bed, and then entered a wholly new
and beautiful region. The road,—such a road as
only French military roads can be,—wound cork-
screw fashion about the hills which were verdant from base to summit. Now we passed
under a natural arch of olive boughs ; now we
came upon a sunny plateau with fields of corn
and orchards of the fig-tree, the wild plum and
the almond on either side. Everywhere smiled
a happy Nature ; everywhere was the evidence
of peace and plenty. As we advanced more
and more into the country, traces of French
civilisation disappeared, and instead of the
straight little houses with their rows of carob-
trees, new church, and handsome drinking
fountain, we saw on every crest and mountain-
top a Kabyle village, looking, I daresay, precisely as a Kabyle village looked a thousand
years ago. Anything more picturesque and
poetic than the scenery of Grand Kabylia cannot be conceived. The lovely hills, purple or
green or golden as the light made them, each
crowned with a compact mass of tiny stone
houses, the deep valleys of tender green, the
lofty rocks bristling with wild cactus, the groves
of majestic olives, the distant panorama of blue

snow-tipped mountains—all these features made a picture not easy to forget.

The road which our brave little horses climbed so gaily, was very solitary, and wound for the most part between a sharp ravine and precipitous rocks, feathered with almond and plum-trees. Now and then we passed a group of men resting with their working implements by the wayside, stalwart, simple, strange-looking beings, who would greet us with a stare, and a word of broken French or Arabic.

At first the comparison of Arab and Kabyle is by no means flattering to the latter. The Arab is always a gentleman by reason of his personal beauty and dignified manner; whilst the Kabyle, with his ragged shirt, leathern apron, ungraceful proportions, and square homely features, could be no more trimmed into dandyism than a camel. But, after a time, all those observers who are of a practical turn will prefer the physique that argues indomitable strength and perseverance to all the elegance in the world, and will side with every writer who has written a panegyric on the Kabyles.

Sometimes a troop of children scampered

down from the heights and followed our
carriage, crying " *Soldi, soldi,*"—brown, well-
grown, wild little things, not so full of frolic
as little Arabs, but able to take a joke very
well.

The journey from the Metidja and ascent
of Fort Napoléon, reminds one of the long ride
across the Campagna to Tivoli. The road
wound round the mountains like a thread
twisted about a sugar-loaf. We looked up,
and said, " Oh ! it is impossible that we can
get there." We looked down, and said, " Have
we really climbed so high ?" And still we
climbed higher and higher and higher. Everywhere were signs of cultivation ; and it was
quite touching to see how laborious, and often
ineffectual, was the system of it.

I wished that I could speak the Berber
tongue, and could lecture an assemblage of
Kabyle farmers upon iron ploughs, and artificial
manure, and team threshing-machines. Their
implements are of the clumsiest kind, precisely
what they were, I daresay, when Numidian
corn filled Roman granaries ; and the effect
of the landscape altogether was to make you
feel carried back to the times of Masinissa,

and to wonder how the place could be so
peaceful.

We were now breathing the brisk mountain
air, and gaining at every moment a wider prospect of the distant peaks of the Djurdjura and
the verdant hills and valleys on every side.
Nothing, perhaps, could be more exhilarating
than such a drive with such an object. The
horses (we employed relays) were fresh, the
temperature was that of a delicious medium
between spring and summer; the scenery was
lovely and quiet, and suggestive of a golden
pastoral life.

It was difficult to conceive what a different
scene we should have traversed only a few
years back. These mountain-passes and lovely
valleys were then alive with the sound of guns
and the flash of swords, and few and far between were the villages that escaped the
scourge of war. The Kabyles, incited by a
fanatic, named Bon Bapla, fought well, but the
sight of their ruined crops and burning olive-
woods sooner than anything else inclined them
to peace, and there seems no likelihood of its
being again broken.

By-and-by, our driver turned round with a

joyful face, and cried, "Voilà Fort Napoléon," and stretching our necks and shading our eyes we did indeed see a white speck on the mountain before us.

A little later, and we drove into the quiet little fort and alighted at the best inn it boasted of, to the infinite amusement of some Kabyles lounging about. Despite some drawbacks, such as a saloon crowded to the last inch with French soldiers playing billiards, Kabyles and all kinds of miscellaneous travellers, tiny bed-rooms, only approached by a staircase built outside, with holes in the roof, in the walls, and in the floor, we made ourselves very comfortable at Fort Napoléon. The landlord and landlady did their best to please us, and after they had served our dinner, chatted to us over their own at the next table. The food was wholesome and the beds were clean.

And we had a very pleasant time. M. le Commandant, to whom we were provided with letters, received us kindly, and with great amiability consented to be looked upon as a sort of encyclopædia concerning Kabyle affairs. He was a pleasant, learned man, who had lived long among the Kabyles, and had busied him-

self with collecting such *disjecta membra* of
their grammatical language as yet remain. It
was delightful to hear him talk of the people,
and their prospects, much as if he were their
father ; and, unassuming though he was, one
could see that he had proved a benefactor to
them. He spoke very hopefully of the Kabyle
arboriculture, and told us that he had found
the people skilful in grafting several kinds of
fruit trees introduced by himself.

When our talk with the Commandant was over,
Madame, accompanied by a young lady, wife
of the *chef du bureau Arabe*, did the honours of
the place. A terrific north wind had arisen since
our arrival, accompanied with heavy showers,
and we felt quite sorry for all the poor ladies
endured in our behalf. We were driven hither
and thither ; our umbrellas were turned inside ;
our faces were all but skinned; it was impossible to stir a step till the blast had passed.
I think one must travel to Fort Napoléon
before understanding what a north wind can
be.

There was a little new church, and a tiny
shop containing groceries and Kabyle pottery;
and a big barracks, and a splendid panoramic

view of the country to see. But what interested us far more just then, was the everyday life at Fort Napoléon, as described by these ladies.

The wife of the *chef du bureau Arabe* was a young, pretty, and elegant lady, who had only left Paris a year or two ago. I naturally asked a question or two concerning the amusements at Fort Napoléon : Were there military concerts, or balls, or pic-nics, or any available gaieties within reach? She gave a little scream of laughter.

"Balls at Fort Napoléon, Madame!" she said, "why, there are only three ladies here, Madame la Commandante, Madame the Captain's wife, and myself! And, unfortunately, we have no band; but we console ourselves as well as we can, and are capital neighbours to each other."

" I daresay you often have visits of friends from Algiers?"

" *Pardon*, Madame, very seldom indeed. It is so far and the journey is so tedious. We are not dull, however, for we have our husbands with us, and a very tranquil life on the whole."

The elder lady was equally philosophical,

F

and both entered with interest into the subject of Kabyle idiosyncrasy and character. It was evident that they had taken pains to learn something of their adopted country, and that they made their exile as bright as was possible. They told us of many and many an incident that had marked their monotonous life like a milestone, always speaking kindly of the Kabyles.

" They are excellent creatures," said the youngest lady, with a pretty *moue* of dissatisfaction,—" if they only washed themselves!"

I think nothing does away with the patented notions of French ladies, sooner than some experience of them in these hill stations. We grow up with the idea that a Frenchwoman is brilliant, elegant, but a plaything only, and with difficulty believe her adapted for a domestic life under circumstances of. peculiar hardship. During my travels in Algeria, I made the acquaintance of many ladies, living in out of the way military stations, and must say, that I never anywhere received such a distinct impression of good wives, careful mothers, and capable as well as graceful housekeepers.

Fortunately, the wind dropped that night, or we should have seen very little of Kabylia. As it was, we woke up to a glorious day, cold but bright, and saw the sun lighting up a thousand soft green valleys and violet peaks tipped with snow.

Which way should we go? Eastward, westward? We descended from the height on which Fort Napoléon stood, neat little roads leading on each side to some eagle-nest of a Kabyle village. Chance led us in the direction of a shady path that wound round the fort, dipped sheer into a valley, and then climbed towards a cluster of cosy little houses, surrounded by fig and olive orchards.

Nothing could equal the variety and magnificence of the scenery that seemed to shift at every turning. The sunny hills crested with villages ; the fair and fruitful fields that lay below ; the distant range of lofty mountains standing out, as if of amethyst, against the cool blue sky. Such a prospect could but make us linger lovingly and regretfully, since we felt we should never see it again.

When we came near the village, a troop of girls and children gathered shyly about us ;

one or two scampered home to tell of our arrival, and by-and-by, we found ourselves in a circle of simple, wandering creatures, all smiling, all shy, and all dumb.

They were for the most part good-looking, with healthful complexions and plenty of intelligence; women and children were dressed alike, in dark blue woollen *haiks*, or shawls some yards in breadth, which were fastened on the shoulders with a brooch and round the waist by a coloured girdle. These garments reached to the ankle, and they wore no kind of shoe. But this clumsy garb was brightened by all kinds of rude jewellery, such as chains, bracelets, and anklets of silver, coral, palm-seeds, shells, coins, glass beads, and berries. The happy mothers of sons were distinguished by a circular brooch, or fibula, of very gay metal-work, fastened in front of their head-dress; and some of the ornaments were really pretty and valuable. Most of them had a cross tattooed on the brow, which is said to be the relic of an early Christian faith once existing among these mountains. After a little, their shyness wore off, and though the French of the whole party amounted to " Bon jour," and the Arabic of our own to six words, we got on very well. The children grinned and gesticulated, the girls tittered, the women examined our dresses, our cloaks, and our hat - strings with enthusiastic wonder.

There was one charming creature about five-and-twenty, who seemed to be the oracle as well as the life of the party. She had bright cheeks and lips, large grey eyes, beaming with intelligence, and a frank, broad brow that told plainly enough how very little education would fit her for the very best kind of civilisation. There was not a hint or shadow of shame in her bright face as she compared our European garb to her own, and evidently our condition too ; for she turned to one of her companions and seemed to sum up a hasty verdict, whether in our favour or her own, we could not tell.

It amused her immensely that we should be so amused, and she plainly thought us a little impertinent for trying to buy some of her neck-laces. Sell her jewels, forsooth, and, least of all, the brooch she wore in honour of having borne her husband a male child; what were we good for, to dream of such absurdities ? This was said as plainly as looks can say rather cutting things; but a moment after, she was all fun, and friendliness again, making the utmost of our precious little store of Arabic, and ready to tell us anything and everything, could we only have understood. Some of the girls held out their hands begging, " Soldi, soldi," but she was far too proud, and when one of us touched her bracelet with a lingering look of admiration, she gave a wicked little "Phew !" as much as to say, "Don't you wish you may get it ?" One or two women were only too eager to sell their ornaments, but expected a handful of money in return.

We wandered about the village, which was not so enticing as it had promised to be. The orchards were fresh and balmy enough, but the interiors had an unsavoury and unwholesome look; there was no appearance of whitewash, and the furniture consisted of a little pottery and some mats. Babies tumbled about among the goats, apparently as uncared for; heaps of refuse pained the eye and ear at every corner, and you felt constrained to look away towards the shiny hills and snowy mountains. Want of cleanliness is in fact the only blot on the idyllic picture of Kabyle life.

As we were returning, a touching incident brought home to us all that we had heard and read of Kabyle hospitality. By the wayside sat a withered old woman, having on her knee a basket of dried figs; she was talking to a fine, stalwart, well-dressed young fellow, who bent over her pityingly, and to me it seemed, rather condescendingly. We stopped to interchange a greeting with them; and finding the young man tolerably conversant with French, were enabled to carry on quite a conversation. The woman stared at us, and prattled about our queer costumes with the simple garrulity of age, but her companion held up his head, and evidently considered a Kabyle equal to a Frank any day. When our chat had come to an end, the kindly old creature doled out her figs to us as a parting gift, evidently delighted at our acceptance of them. Of course the figs were worth a sou or two only, but she had nothing else to give, and evidently could ill afford them, so that we had double right to be grateful.

Tourists bring home carved ivory from Dieppe, mosaics from Florence, and pottery or arms from Kabylia. The pottery (of which

there are now specimens in the South Ken-
sington Museum) is quaint, and highly interesting, whether you consider it from the artistic or
manufacturer's point of view: Water-jars, vases,
lamps, dishes, and an infinite variety of vessels
either for use or ornament, were to be had in
the little general shop at Fort Napoléon, and,
for the most part, at nominal prices.   This
ware is all of dark rich red and yellow, pat-
terned in black.   No two pieces of pottery or
patterns are precisely alike; and both design
and manipulation of the clay are the work of
women.   It is said that those women who excel
in this art are much esteemed, however they
may be wanting in grace or loveliness—which
certainly speaks a good deal for Kabyle common sense.

I have read somewhere that a Kabyle was
one day selling a beautiful lamp, and some
vases, when a neighbour came up, and cried
in his enthusiasm,—

"By the head of the Prophet, I would give
a thousand douros for a woman with such
taste!"

"You shall have her for the half," said
the merchant, and without ado he brought the

poor artist forward. She was, however, so ugly, that the lover of fine art took to his heels.

The colours are fixed on the clay by means of resin, mixed with a little olive oil, and which, as the earth is yellowish to begin with, forms the yellow. The red is given by an ochre, found in the country; and for the black, they have recourse to fat or resinous bodies in ignition. With such simple materials it is marvellous what pretty things these Kabyle women produce; and they do not confine themselves to the ornamental only, making pipkins for cooking, large jars for oil, and all kinds of smaller ones for honey, butter, and milk.

The arms and weapons were no less interesting to us, though less easy to purchase and bring home, being heavy, and of course expensive in comparison to the pottery. These rude mountaineers have certainly had a village Ruskin among them at some time or another, to inculcate the worship of the Beautiful. Not an implement of whatever metal or make, but was ornamented wherever ornamentation was possible; and we unwillingly left behind us a beautiful but cumbersome gun, to be had for a hundred francs. It was most curiously and artistically worked, and richly inlaid with coral. Short daggers were to be had in plenty, of very bad metal for the most part, though valuable on account of the workmanship and taste displayed.

Chapter 6.

CHARACTER OF THE KABYLES.—LEGEND AND HISTORY.—
THE KABYLE TRÈVE DE DIEU.—MOUNTAIN HEROINES.—
ASPECTS OF KABYLE LIFE.

HERE is something quite touching in the primitive life of these mountaineers, and there are a few things in such records of it as we possess, that I think must be interesting to student as well as tourist.

Living, in the midst and yet utterly apart from Roman, Turk, and Arab, the Kabyle or Berber has preserved his identity through successive ages, as much as the soil of which he is native. From the earliest history we find him loving liberty and contesting with his oppressors, till, driven to the Djurdjura or *Mons Ferratus*, he defied them, and built houses, tilled fields, and enjoyed the plenty of the land in peace. He is said to have been a better Christian than he has become a Mahometan, and to show unmistakable inclinations towards the religion to which his forefathers were converted under Roman rule. Indeed, near Fort Napoléon, there is a village whose chiefs, having studied the Gospel under the curé, —desired the privilege of baptism ; and if we may believe all those enthusiastic writers who have made the Kabyles their study, the women will ere long forego the tattoo on their brows for the sign of the cross, of which it is said to be a remembrance.

But far more interesting than any myth is the organization of Kabyle society as we find it to-day, and should have found it, I daresay, had we lived in ante-Islam times.

The poorest Kabyle village is said to offer the interesting spectacle of a real political life, active, democratic, republican. The little community chooses its magistrates, taxes itself, levies and repeals imposts, in fine, forms a kind of savage little Switzerland, neither wanting in graver nor lesser interests of responsible parliamentary government.

Sometimes there are scenes in these village debates as stormy as those which took place at the time of the Great Remonstrance. Wordy wars ensue. A gun is fired. The whole village rushes to arms, and anarchy prevails for awhile. And the power of the chief is so very conditional that the least abuse of authority on his part calls forth a distinct and fierce defiance. " Enta chikh, ana chikh," a sturdy Kabyle will say to his superior when indignant; which literally translated is, " You chief—I chief," and expresses the most unconditional equality.

Every village is led by a code of traditional laws called *kanoun*, which many writers consider as derived from the Greek word κανὼν, and a vague remembrance of the ecclesiastical canons of the religion to which the Kabyles formerly belonged. These *kanoun* are handed down from old to young, and differ in every village.

Here are some of the laws of Kabylia :—

	Fr.	Cent.
The young man who insults an old man shall pay	1	60
The chief, who by cowardice makes peace without considering the honour of his village, shall pay	300	
He who interposes between two persons, one of whom has a legitimate vengeance to inflict on the other, pays	200	

	Fr.	Cent.
He who appropriates to himself the meat set aside for the poor pays		50
He who appropriates to himself the arms of any stranger who has died fighting in the village, covers himself with dishonour and pays	125	
He who insults a woman pays	1	60
He who troubles the order of the public assembly	7	20

These extracts from the *Codex Kabyliæ* suggest a good deal of rather fierce but honest humanity, and give an index to the national character. Unbounded pride, patriotism, and charity to the poor prevail, whilst, it must be admitted, that the veto in any kind of interference between murder is somewhat savage. Indeed, though they do not go so far as to echo the Koran, and proscribe "an eye for an eye and a tooth for a tooth," they encourage a system of vendetta, the practice of which is a very good apology for capital punishment.

The murderer ceases to belong to his tribe, and his goods are confiscated, but the friends of the victim are allowed, nay, are expected to take their bloody revenge. If the inheritor of the frightful privilege be a woman, she hires her murderer.

But there are one or two institutions of the

Kabyle society that go far to remedy all other short-comings. The first of these is the *Anaya,* a touching custom something like the *Grid* of the Scandinavians, and the *trève de Dieu* of the Normans. It is somewhat difficult to define, but worthy the notice of any one interested in the Kabyles and their customs.

The *Anaya* is alike a law and a tradition. It represents a city of refuge to the guilty, a protection to the weak, a talisman of safety to the wanderer; it stands in good stead of treaties, ambassadors, and diplomacy; it is a mere name, and yet it is stronger and more sacred than any sovereignty of which we know.

The *Anaya,* says General Daumas, is the sultan of the Kabyles. A Kabyle will abandon his wife, his children, his country; he never abandons his Anaya.

This singular custom may be described as a contract of inviolability between individuals, families, and tribes. The pledge of it, which may be a dog, a gun, a knife, or any trifle consecrated by the name of its possessor, is sacred to all, and can be given by all, carries the bearer of it safe through a hostile region, accords him the right of asylum if he be a criminal, of hospitality if he be a traveller, of mercy and kindness and protection under any circumstances. In fact, the *Anaya* acts as a kind of freemasonry, and may be compared to freemasonry. Excepting in one or two particulars, it exists for all irrespective of sex. The Kabyles, as you see, like the primitive Norse people, treat their women like reasonable beings.

Next in importance and originality to the *Anaya* is the institution of the *Zaonïa*, which represents, in one word, the cultivation of letters, the conservation of faith, the instruction of youth, and the care of the poor. Here, in a collection of buildings all under one roof, the pious teach the Koran and the Conversations of the Prophet; here the learned give instruction in grammar and versification. Here the poor and the friendless find shelter and food; and here the saintly find a grave. In some Zaonïas, outcasts are made welcome indeed to stay, and in none, are they refused temporary relief; even the stray ass or mule is housed and fed.

The enormous expenses of these monastic-

like institutions are defrayed by various re-
venues, such as the contributions of pilgrims,
legacies, presents from the parents of pupils,
lands, flocks and herds. Moreover, there is
always some learned priest or marabout presiding over a Zaonïa, who purchases divine
favours for the faithful, and of course does
not go unrewarded. When a pupil leaves
the home of his youth to go into the world,
his masters assemble, and one reads the
Fatah, or opening prayer of the Koran, over
him :—

" Praise be to God, Lord of the Universe :
" The merciful, the pitiful.
" O Judge of the day of retribution,
" It is Thee we adore, Thy help we beg !
" Direct us in the right path :
" In the path of those whom Thou hast
laden with Thy benefits.
" Not of those who have incurred Thy
displeasure, or have gone from the right
way."

The youth thanks them and repeats this
formula :—

" Oh, my masters, you have taught me,
giving yourselves much trouble on my account.

G

If I have caused you pain, I ask your pardon at the moment of separation."

Surely a simple and touching farewell to the *Alma Mater* which has nourished him!

The *soff*, which is something like the *fœdus* of the Etruscans, is also well worthy of notice. A *soff* is the alliance of men, villages, and tribes, sometimes united with a view to escape oppression, sometimes to exact reprisals; it may exist in peace or war; may have been organized yesterday or ages past, and may be broken or changed to-morrow. It is curious that among some tribes guns were exchanged in times of peace, and if any cause for quarrel arose, the pledge would be recalled. This custom reminds one of the Roman herald, who was sent to shoot an arrow into a hostile country as a symbol of war.

A word about the poor and the women, and I have done.

The Kabyles entertain the real Mahometan faith in almsgiving, and do not regard poverty as a vice, but as an accident. The poor in their turn do not cant or cringe, but say their say, and state their wants, without a blush or an excuse.

"Those who bestow alms," says the Prophet, "whether in public or in private, shall be rewarded of God. Fear shall not overtake them and they shall not be afflicted."

And again, "Render to thy neighbours that which is their due, and also to the poor and the traveller."

And again : "Oh, believers, do not make your alms worthless by reproaches or evil conduct, as doth he who gives largely from ostentation, and does not believe in God or the last day."

The Kabyles are lax Mahometans as regards eating the flesh of wild boar, keeping Ramadhan, and saying their daily prayers, but they certainly do not fall short in their obligations to the poor. Every now and then a certain sum is taken out of the public treasury and laid out in meat, which the poor partake of in public. This generally takes place on the occasion of great religious fête or national celebration, and is called *ouzia*.

If a cow or an ox meet its death by accident,

the owner is not at liberty to dispose of it, till he has first distributed a portion to the sick and feeble in the village.

After a marriage, and the birth or circumcision of a son, there are always fêtes, and all the fragments of the feast are the property of the poor. They manage these things better in Kabylia. How often are not the remnants of a snobbish London dinner-party served next day to poor relations or unimportant acquaintances!

On the whole the Kabyles treat their women pretty well. True, that she is sold to her husband after a sort of appraisement, and can inherit no property, but she takes her place as wife and mother in the house, has no rivals, eats with her lord, and goes unveiled to market or the fountain. It would seem that the Kabyle women are made of very good stuff, for we read of them inciting their husbands and brothers to battle, much after the fashion of the Scandinavian women described by Tacitus; and in some cases become female marabouts.

The story of Lalla-Fatima-bent-ech-Sheik will show what a Kabyle heroine can be. This Lalla-Fatima, who was born in a Zouave village in the interior, and for aught I know is living in exile now, is an extraordinary combination of a Boadicea, a Dorcas, a Druidess, and a Zenobia. She headed an insurrection against the French; she was revered for her charities from one end of the country to the other; she excelled in divination; and she bore capture and exile nobly.

A Kabyle poet has composed a ballad of somewhat melancholy turn, relating the biography of this wonderful woman, whose fame is spread far and wide.

Of course, it was not in the nature of things for even a female revolutionist to be let alone by the French Government, and Lalla-Fatima expiates her ambition far away from her native mountains.

There are other saints and warriors of the female sex, hardly less celebrated, and Kabyle history abounds in legends respecting them. One unfortunate tribe, that of Aith-Bou-Akkach, is embroiled in inevitable war to this day, on account of a curse called down upon it by a saint named Lalla Kadijah. She was descending from the hills one day on horseback, when all the village was assembled upon public affairs. The young people looked a little impertinently at the holy Amazon, and one irreverent youth so far forgot himself as to point to a wretched old beggar and cry, " Ho-la, Lalla ! Are you come to marry old grand-papa here ?"

At which, the people, instead of reproving him, laughed.

The female marabout grew furious and said, " You will suffer for it, ungodly parents that you are, for letting your children rail against woman's grey hairs. May the curse of Heaven light on you! May no year pass over your tribe without some war disturbing your peace!"

And even in her grave Lalla Kadijah incites the devil to work woe among the sons of Aith-Bou-Akkach.

But what is far more interesting than these stories of the famous, is the life of ordinary men and women in Kabylia as described by those French writers who have seen it.

When the toil of the day is over, the women make their toilette, arraying themselves in their jewellery; neighbours and friends assemble at the house-doors, and chat or sing to the accompaniment of flutes; all is sociability and rustic enjoyment. Putting a background of blue hills, olive-groves, fruit-gardens, and a summer sky, this makes a pretty picture.

Chapter 7.

IF the great feast of the Ramadhan is gloomy and depressing, at least it comes in and goes out gaily enough. The Negroes choose the opportunity of decking themselves out and driving through the town, their houris put on silks and gauzes, and dance all night, their wise women practise a barbarous kind of Fetishism on the sea-shore; while the Moorish ladies make an infinity of sweets and pasties, and invite all their lady friends to a feast.

The Negroes being a very sociable set of people, it is much easier to join in their gaieties than in those of the secluded Moors. I am, therefore, indebted to them for my share in the festivities preceding Ramadhan. Why the Negroes, who still practise a strange sort

of Fetishism brought from the Sahara, should
dance out their evil spirits, and propitiate their
demons at this particular time, I don't know;
but upon any and every public holiday or
rejoicing, you are sure to hear their music and
see their finery.

A few days before Ramadhan, we were guided
by a nice old Negress wrapt in blue drapery
to a Moorish house in the old town, where we
were assured some beautiful things were to be
seen. As we passed through the dark passage
leading to the court, one or two Negresses
were coming out, and their nudge and look, as
promising amusement, were very encouraging.

We found the court, as usual, open to the
sky, and despite the crowds thronging it on
every side, not unbearably warm. In the
centre was a group of Negresses, dressed in
flimsy muslins and gauzes, whilst the gallery
looking upon the court was crowded with
Arabs, Jews, Zouaves, French soldiers, and
miscellaneous spectators. A miserable little
calf, to be sacrificed and afterwards eaten, lay
in a dark corner; and as we made our way
along, we could hardly help treading on some
poor fowls, tied by the legs, that lay here and

there, awaiting the same fate. A band of musicians, with an expression of the utmost solemnity upon their shining black faces, sat on the floor, making just the sort of music to give healthy people an idea of neuralgic agonies. Indeed, mild toothache is a pleasing pain compared with the endurance inflicted by the Negro, who feels himself all the more important, and all the more likely of extra payment, for being noisy. He has brought from the Soudan a taste for those terrible iron casta-gnettes, called *keg-ka-kef,* a word derived from the sound evoked from them; and if any one will take the trouble to get the Sunday-school children of his parish to repeat this word till they are hoarse, he will have some idea of it.

Finding ourselves a little too much elbowed, and being affectionately invited up-stairs by every Negress who could get near enough to nudge us, we climbed two pair of winding stone steps, and saw the rest of the perform-ances from the terrace.

We had the top of the house all to our-selves, which was a great comfort, and, though the sun was warm, and the brilliant light of the surrounding white roofs glaring, the air was blue and fresh, as if Negroes were not within miles. For though I like Negroes very much, and found them obliging, and the babies enchanting little things, I must confess that they carry a personality with them as perceptible to the ear as their black personality is to the eye.

Irrespective of the sight below, the terrace was picturesque and interesting enough to have kept us there a little while. The blue mountain line in the distance, the bits of foliage breaking the white mountains of the house-roofs here and there, the dark-eyed Moorish girls peeping over the neighbouring walls, the flowers and fruit-trees trellised about us, all these formed a new and curious picture.

But the wonderful music from below, and the dancing that accompanied it, compelled our attention. The dance was by no means ungraceful, and consisted in undulating movements of the arms and body, whilst the music recommended itself by an unintermittent succession of surprises. For it is impossible to get used to Negro music. What affected you like galvanism yesterday, affects you no less to-day ; what sent a thrill of unexpected horrors through every fibre of your body five minutes ago, will have just the same effect a quarter of an hour hence.

We were inclined to endure any torments, moreover, for the sake of the curious and mystic ceremonies to come. Who could help wishing to see the sacrifices, horrid as they might be? One thought of the grand old Greek times, with the fancy that here there might be something to remind one of the goats without blemish, or of the firstling lambs offered to Phœbus Apollo in Homeric story.

But the poor little calf in the corner, which had no sort of dignity about it, being bony and bristly, and altogether un-Homeric, was kept as the *bonne bouche* of the entertainment—which we did not see. Hour after hour passed, dancer after dancer fell back exhausted on her seat, and we kept asking, " When is the sacrifice to take place ?" when at last patience gave way, and we went home, wondering as to the long endurance of people who were content to dance and sing, and voluntarily torment themselves for twelve hours in succession.

These dances are not nearly so weird and
fanciful as other Negro ceremonies that precede
the great Fast.

These ceremonies take place on the sea-
shore, and are too extraordinary not to attract
every stranger in Algiers. Morning after
morning, every omnibus bound to the pretty
suburban village of St. Eugène, is filled to
the last corner with Negresses carrying cocks
to the sacrifice, with Jewish and Moorish
women dressed in their best, and with inquisitive spectators like ourselves, intent upon
seeing everything.

By eight o'clock one fresh morning, we
were rattling away towards St. Eugène. In
company with us was a handsome Quadroon
woman, carrying a pair of miserable chickens,
and an Arab and his wife, all evidently very
serious about the impending ceremony, and
the part they were to take in it. In a quarter
of an hour we felt the brisk breezes blowing off
the Mediterranean, and alighted to find ourselves in a scene wholly new and almost indescribable.

The bit of coast selected for the ceremonies
reminded me of Cornwall. A line of dark

rocks, broken into stepping-stones where the tide was low, a little cove of glistening white sand here, a delicious rise of bright green turf there, a perspective of shelving cliffs and creamy billows—except for the aloes, I could have fancied myself at the Lizard.

Descending a steep path that wound amid a hollow to the shore, we were at once plunged into the midst of sorceries and mysticisms past counting. For the first few minutes the colour only, and no hidden meaning of the scene, was plain to us. We felt as if we had hitherto been blind, the purples, and reds, and yellows seemed so near our eyes. This distinctness of each separate bit of brilliancy had never struck me in the same degree before; perhaps because this was the first time I had ever seen such a variety of complexion and costume in bright sunlight. The Quadroons with their lustrous gold-brown skins and blue drapery, the Jewesses with their black hair and crimson brocades, the little Moorish girls with their crocus-coloured shawls, pink trousers, and fingers dyed rose colour with henna, the Negresses with their black cheeks and green *haiks*, I had seen a hundred times, but never before assem-

bled against a background of bright blue sea
and sky.

We descended the hollow slowly, im-
patiently elbowed by believers in the Djinns
or spirits, here to be exorcised or appeased.
The spot itself is consecrated to seven Djinns
presiding over seven springs, the waters of
which are held to be of miraculous effect.
Very likely there is as much of science as
superstition in this, for mineral springs of real
efficacy are found elsewhere in Algeria.

There were many priestesses in this strange
worship—witch-like old Negresses, who wrought
all their magic by the aid of a caldron, a
handful of fire, and a little incense. Rows of
tiny wax-lights were stuck in the ground
before them, and here childless wives paid a
few sous, sipped the enchanted water, and
went away believing in the advent of future
sons; garments of sick people were miraculously
endued with the power of healing, children
were cured of burns and bruises, cripples
were cured of rheumatism, and lovers of
coldness. Even one or two Frenchwomen
were come to ensure themselves some boon
not obtainable in a legitimate way.

Leaving the Moorish enchantresses, we next turned to the Negro priests, old men in tattered shirts, seated amid crowds of devotees, and each forming the centre of a cruel and curious scene. Once fairly among these tatterdemalion brothers of Calchas, we found it impossible to stir a step or glance in any direction without the contact of newly shed blood. It was horrid. The bright red stains were everywhere, crimsoned feathers were blown in our faces, and from the time we came to that of departure, hapless cocks, some half killed without intermission, and thrown towards the sea. If the poor creatures flutter sea-ward in their dying struggle, the omen is propitious, and the women shout their horrid *yoo, yoo, yoo* of joy; but if they flutter landward, another pair of fowls is swung backward and forward by the priest, incantations are muttered over it, and the sacrifice is performed afresh. There were goats also, which met the same fate, and were skinned and cut up in indescribable haste, destined, as well as the cocks, to furnish the feast at night.

It was past ten o'clock when we left. Negroes, Moors, and Jews, were still flocking to the sacrifice; but the sight was not a lovely one, and we had seen enough of it.

A few days after this, Ramadhan began. The firing of a cannon inaugurated it, at sound of which children clapped their little hands and shouted for joy, old men embraced each other, and not a Mussulman but expressed a certain kind of dignified satisfaction.

Of course it is very difficult to measure the significance of this great institution, the Fast of Ramadhan, the third fundamental base of Islamism as established by Mahomet. Prayer, almsgiving, fasting, pilgrimage, and the profession of faith, are the five indispensable principles of Mahometan worship; and the third, naturally enough, attracts the stranger more than any.

"Oh, believers," says the Prophet, "fasting is prescribed to you, as it was prescribed to those who came before you. Fear the Lord.

"The month of Ramadhan in which the Koran descended from on high to serve as a guide to men, as a clear explanation of precepts, and distinction between good and evil, is the time of fasting. He who is ill or on a journey shall fast an equal number of days afterwards.

H

" It is permitted to you to eat and drink till the moment when you can distinguish a white thread from a black one. From that time observe the fast strictly till night."

Women who are *enceinte*, or nursing infants, imbeciles, young children, and very old men are permitted to eat, the latter on condition that they give a little corn to the poor.

The fast is broken at sunset, when a cannon sounds, and the Moorish cafés begin to fill. You see little cups of coffee handed round, and after awhile the stolid silence melts, and the tall white-draped figures sitting round look a little less like statues.

During the day-time it is impossible not to notice the look of depression pervading the old town. The industrious little embroiderers whom I noticed in the second chapter, get so faint about noon-time that they are sent home ; and of course the general physique suffers enormously from such a sacrifice imposed upon it. That there is a spiritual as well as a material purification intended in this ordinance, is sufficiently made evident by the word Ramadhan, which signifies fire which purifies. It is not enough for believers to abstain from

fleshly gratifications; they must also abstain
from every lie and evil thought, and must not
sin either with the ears, with the tongue, with
the hands, or with the feet.

Nothing in our religion is more impressive
than the ceremony of evening worship during
Ramadhan. The mosques are all lighted up;
Turks, Moors, and Arabs flock thither in
crowds; the fountains are thronged with the
poor, who perform their ablutions, and the outer
courts with beggars, the lame, the halt, and
the blind, who moan and mourn, and hold out
their hands alike to Mussulman and Roumi.

Leaving the streets and passing through
an avenue of these importunate and wretched
creatures, I have found myself many and many
a time in a scene almost impossible to realize
now, and how much more impossible to describe!

One's first experience is that of being in a
garden. Those trickling fountains, those clusters of banana and palmetto, those dusky skies
studded with brilliant stars, are surely no accessories of a temple. But a few steps farther
on, and a forest of aisles break upon the eye,
the white domes lighted by lamps not too

thickly hung, the pavements covered with soft carpet, the columns countless in number, and exquisitely proportioned.

The loftiness, the immensity, and the partial light of these domes and arcades, cannot fail to be very impressive; but if the outer courts of the temple strike one with an involuntary feeling of solemnity, how much more shall do so the temple itself!

Picture to yourself a broad or dimly-lighted aisle with rows of worshippers on their faces, the elegantly dressed Moor beside the ragged Biskri, the Bedouin, the Negro, and the Turk, united in the common act of prayer. The colours of their dress, the lines of their figures, the mingled sounds of their voices as they chant the sacred Litany, omitting no gesture ordained by the Prophet, have something strange and weird in this solemn sort of twilight, whilst the leading voice of the Imam, from a high pulpit opposite, seems to come from an unearthly distance. But it is impossible to give any idea of such a scene. The lights and shadows are too dim, the outlines too vast, the accessories too difficult, to realize with any words.

It is like the dream of a Mahometan millennium when the temple serves for all worshippers, and yet there is space for more. One must live in Mahometan countries to realize the inherent connexion between Mahomet's religion and the people and country to whom he bequeathed it. One must study the Arabs, too, before talking of converting them to Christianity.

The attitudes of prayer are numerous and striking,* and are well suggested in the frontispiece. Here we have the first and last action of the litany, which opens and concludes with the words, " Allah—Akbar. God is great." The third figure, receding as if on his palms, performs an action of private or supplementary prayer. The background is a sketch of the beautiful Mosque in the Rue de la Marine, Algiers.

When Ramadhan comes to an end, the streets of Algiers are like the scenes of some gay *féerie* at the Porte St. Martin.

The Negroes dance through the town to the sound of castanet and drum, wearing bright-

---

* See Lane's " Modern Egyptians," ch. iii. p. 76.

coloured clothes and flowers stuck behind their ears. The Moorish ladies pay visits dressed in diaphanous drapery of silky white with sashes of crimson and gold, and their Negresses follow leading by the hand some dainty little Omar or Zorah, its tiny fingers dyed with henna, and its tiny body decked in purple and orange. Every one is busy on pleasure, and if you drop into a bazaar, you find the merchant seated in the midst of his friends enjoying a grave kind of hilarity.

Monsieur L——, the good-natured *interprète judiciaire*, who had become my instructor in Arabic, was kind enough to take me with his wife upon a round of morning calls at this time. It was the best, and at the same time the worst opportunity possible for visiting Moorish families; for you might as well try to catch a Jew dull at a bargain as a Moorish gentleman or lady unoccupied during the week after Ramadhan. We were fortunate, however, to find the very persons we most wanted to see at home, and though the lady was busy preparing for friends, we were entreated to stay and partake of coffee. The host, a gentlemanly handsome man of forty, received us with that exquisite charm of manner which is Arab *par excellence*, and introduced us to his three children, boys whose ages varied from five to fifteen. The eldest, named Hassan, was a slim, delicate youth, dressed in vest and several drawers of pale mauve, who spoke French perfectly, talked to me of the Fenians, of foreign travel, and of his own prospects with much intelligence and no spark of hobbledehoyish embarrassment. The youngest named Omar, a rosy little fellow with roguish black eyes, kissed us prettily, though he didn't much like it, and then stood at his father's knee biting his henna-tipped fingers, and quizzing us to his heart's content.

We sat in an elegant room, blooming with soft carpets, coloured lamps, brackets painted with flowers and arabesques, and tiny-looking glasses framed in silver and gems. In an alcove stood a bed hung with magnificent curtains of white silk embroidered with gold, and beside it a table of inlaid mother-of-pearl. Before us was a pretty little court, whose delicate marble pillars, flowers and fountain, refreshed the eye after the superabundance of colour within, whilst stately Negresses moved indolently about with brush and broom, making pretence to be busy.

We talked of many things, but mostly of the prospects of these three boys. Our host, whose face had grown familiar to me at the Governor-General's receptions, and who filled an important official post in Algiers, spoke openly of his perplexities on that head.

"That boy there," he said, smilingly indicating his eldest son, "wants, like everybody else now-a-days, to see the world. He must be a barrister (*avocat*), I think, and go to Paris. If I make a doctor of him, he will get few patients among the Arabs, and none among the French. Trade is no longer a road to fortune. It is very difficult to obtain anything worth having under the government. My boys do not labour under the disadvantage that I have done, and must turn their French education to good purpose somehow, but how? *Voilà la difficulté.*"

Hassan laughed gaily, thinking, I dare say, how pleasant it would be to see Paris and become a man of the world.

"I shall see England, too, shan't I, father?" he said, and when I promised to show him something in London whenever he came so far, he laughed more gaily still.

A Negress now appeared at the doorway bearing coffee and cake on a massive gold salver. Hassan sprang to take it of her, and setting it on the floor served us with tiny cups of delicious coffee, each being handed in an outer cup of delicate silver filigree work.

Nothing could exceed the cheerfulness and cordiality of this interesting family, and the visit would have been delightful but for one drawback. Whenever I was brought into contact with Moorish domestic life, the degraded position of the women struck me painfully, but never so painfully as now. Here were all the accessories of a happy home, the refinements of wealth, graceful intelligent children, an amiable, worthy, and polished man at the head; but the mother was nothing. We naturally asked after Madame, with many regrets at not being able to see her.

"Madame," said our host, "is occupied; and moreover, like most Moorish ladies, does not speak French. It is not wonderful that she is a little backward in coming forward. To you English ladies," he added, turning to me, " who travel so much, I daresay it seems surprising that our ladies can live, keeping within doors as they constantly do ; it is the custom, not a good custom, but *on s'y habitue*;" and then he dropped the subject as if it were a painful one.

Chapter 8.

JOURNEY TO THE CEDAR FOREST.— CROSSING THE METIDJA.
—PREPARATIONS FOR A BRIDAL.— CALLS OF CEREMONY
AND A BALL.— SLEEPING IN A CARAVAN.

N the 6th of March, 1866, I set off in company with four friends towards the cedar-forest of Teniet-el-Haad. We made Blidah our starting-point, and having sent on relays, performed the journey of a hundred and fifty miles in slow and pleasant fashion, neither tiring ourselves, nor our drivers, nor our horses.

The weather was bright but cold, and when we left the plain behind us and began to ascend, north winds and storms of rain compelled us to bring out our wraps and draw the curtains of our cars as close as might be. So cold was it, indeed, that for the most part we contented ourselves with a peep at the scenery now and

then, though such scenery would have been a
treat for the eye at any other time.

After leaving the glorious and historic plain
of the Metidja—I say glorious advisedly, for to
me there is a positive glory in the light and
shadow, the purple and gold, the infinite lines,
the tender nestlings of towns, the quietude, and
breadth, and variety of this or any large plain—
we wound amid a picturesque mountain country till we came to Milianah, our first halt.
Milianah has the most imposing site of any
town I know.   Perched midway between
mountain and mountain, one bold peak tower-
ing above it, its walls white as marble, its background purple and green, a sunbeam suffices
to turn the distant prospect of Milianah into
a pomp and pageantry not easy to forget.
Around are mountains of varied outline and
colour, some round, and soft, and of mossy green
or velvety violet, others sharp and sierra-like,
and of steely grey, and all seen on a day of
passing cloud and sunlight, are doubly beautiful.

Beyond Milianah, the mountains divide,
opening the way for the plain which stretches
below bright and broad, a very lake of green-

ness as far as the eye can reach. This view
reminded me of that seen from the Salzburg
hills, only the beauty of the Salzkammergut is
softer and more tender. It is like comparing
real tigers with those in Mr. Leighton's picture
of the Syracusan Bride.

But it was so cold. "The owl, for all his
feathers, was a-cold;" and though every inn in
the town was filled to the last corner with
French officers, we were allowed to warm ourselves at a blazing wood fire, with a promise of
dinner by-and-by, and perhaps beds afterwards.
We did get dinner, and a very good one too,
after waiting till all the hungry officers had
been served; and when we had done, the landlady and her troop of waiters in white blouses
sat down to theirs.

Next day we amused ourselves after a somewhat novel fashion. Early in the morning, the
sous-préfet, to whom we had an introductory
letter, paid us a visit. He was a grave, pleasant man, past middle age, and equally ready
to offer us hospitality and information. When
breakfast was over he carried us off to see his
wife and daughters. The *prefecture* was an
old Moorish house, full of beautiful Moorish

things, such as carpets, lamps, and arms, some
of which were the spoils of Smalas, and of
recent acquisition.

The *sous-préfet's* lady was well dressed, and
a coquette, and had not much conversation;
but her daughters, who wore brown serge and
looked pretty nevertheless, proved lively enough.
The young ladies amused their leisure with
turnery, whilst the *sous-préfet* amused his own
with wool-work.   We were, therefore, shown
the atelier of the first, and the slippers and sofa
cushions of the last.   I often think of that
melancholy *sous-préfet* sorting out his wools and
counting his stitches with no little wonder as to
the degree of *ennui* that could be so relieved.

Having showed us their pretty garden, full
of Eastern plants and palm-trees, the ladies
took us on a round of visits to Moorish families
of their acquaintance.   The first house we
visited belonged to an Agha of great wealth
and importance, and all the ladies of his family
were preparing for a wedding to take place that
evening.   What with the Agha's four wives,
married and unmarried daughters and daughters-
in-law, it was a little difficult to understand the
relationship of the numerous ladies who crowded

round us, offering their faces like children to
be kissed.

We were at once introduced to the bride, a
pretty demure little creature of thirteen. She
was squatted on the floor, and in such a
costume that it was difficult to believe she
could be anything but a doll. Her neck and
shoulders were literally covered with gold neck-
laces and chains ; and her little brown legs,
which were bare from the knee, had silver
anklets. The dress of embroidered vest, gauze
sleeves, and full white cotton drawers, was pretty
enough, but the incongruous mass of ornaments
and the patches of black paint disfiguring her
fresh cheeks spoiled all.

Being conducted to the apartments on the
opposite side of the court, we found ourselves
literally dazzled by the blaze of colour and
gold.

It was the dressing-room of the ladies preparing for the festival, and a troop of dark-
eyed, girlish creatures surrounded us, laugh-
ing, romping, and tittering as they made their
wonderful toilettes. Their purples, their orange,
their crimsons, and blues, made up such a flush
of colour as I never saw. One, a lovely little

thing, with rosy cheeks and large melancholy black eyes, came up, dragging by the button a superb vest of deep carmine colour, heavy with gold braid. Another was clasping necklace after necklace of coral, and amber, and gold over her chemisette of white silk gauze. A third was adjusting a Tunis sash of delicate blue interwoven with silver. A fourth was merrily submitting to a process of hairdressing, at the hands of a Negress dressed in crocus-coloured cotton. All were as merry as children out of school, excepting the first mentioned, with the large eyes, whose name was Hanyfa. Hanyfa was sad, her companions said, because she had lost her baby, and her husband did not find her pretty.

One of the youngest and merriest of the girls brought this recreant youth before us, introducing him after a cool fashion,—

"Here is the youth who finds one of his father's wives prettier than his own !" she said, whereupon every one laughed but ourselves and Hanyfa.

"Is it really true ?" asked the *sous-préfet's* daughter, in a breath ; "for shame, Hassan, your wife is really pretty !"

But Hassan still stuck to his text. He didn't think so, he said, *voilà tout!* He was an effeminate-looking youth of about sixteen, and seemed to have nothing better to do than loiter outside the women's apartments, and talk nonsense.

After a little further entertainment we kissed the ladies all round, and took leave. When halfway downstairs a Negress came running after us with a tray of cakes and sweetmeats; and to gratify her and the family hospitality in general, we went away eating.

We next visited the ladies of a still richer Agha, but a daughter of the house had lately died, and all was silence and mourning. The Agha himself was at Algiers, and we afterwards learned that he had a wife there to whom he granted his company half the year. The wife to whom we were now introduced was a gentle and loving creature, about twenty-eight; pale, oval-faced, and with features of extraordinary refinement, she interested me more than any Moorish lady I had yet seen.

After a little talk, managed by our three or four sentences of Arabic and signs, the lady's daughter and daughter-in-law came in

I

to see us. Then coffee and quince-jelly were handed round, our hostess telling us, when we praised the latter, that it was of her own making.

Moorish ladies, like Eve, always seem busy " on hospitable thoughts intent," when-ever you visit them; and there is something quite touching in the way they sit by, try-ing to catch the meaning of a French word here and there, and, without doubt, quite aware of their own imperfect education and comparative servitude. We talked of our families at home, of European customs, and of a score of domestic matters. One of our party, who had long golden hair, was begged to let it down; and when the Moorish ladies saw the mass of it, the colour of it, and the silkiness of it, they had no words for their admiration.

Hardly was the excitement of this little in-cident over, when we heard an infantine crow close at hand, and looking up, beheld the prettiest mite of an Ayesha held by a young Negress dressed in brilliant green. The child with its little henna-tipped fingers, and the nurse with her dark face and gay dress, made quite a picture as they rested in the doorway, their shadows falling on the white colonnade of the court.

Little Ayesha was very willing to be kissed and played with, but soon cried to be taken by her young grandmamma, our interesting hostess.

When she had been sent away, her mother brought from an inner room a life-size photograph, and put it into our hands, saying, with no little show of pride and affection, " Voilà mon beau-père."

What was my surprise to find that the grandfather of little Ayesha and the husband of our pretty hostess, was no other than the handsome, gentlemanly, well-informed Moor at whose house I had lunched a few days ago! I looked at the portrait again and again, but there was no possibility of being deceived ; and the discovery spoiled both pictures of Moorish domestic life.

I felt too much sympathy with the wife whose acquaintance I had just made, not to resent the ignominy of her position; and I think she read my thoughts. She looked proudly and sorrowfully at her husband's portrait, too, as if glad to belong to him, but sorry that some one else belonged to him as well.

We made our adieux in quite a friendly fashion, and amused ourselves for the rest of the day in sketching and strolling about the town. Madame, the préfet's wife, did not care for walking, however, and soon quitted us, with a parting charge to see her daughters safely to their own door.

"It is not *comme il faut*," she said, "for young ladies to be seen in the streets without a *chaperon;* as the town is always full of officers, it doesn't do, you understand!"

Here was a parody on European emancipation of thought! We were pitying the seclusion and trammels of Moorish ladies, and found out that young Frenchwomen of twenty-three and twenty-four are not trusted alone beyond their own garden! Surely an Arab satirist might make something of such a state of things!

After dinner the préfet sent some officers to conduct us to a ball at the Theatre. Pleasant, dashing fellows are these French officers, ready to take up any new amusement that comes in the way, to make themselves agreeable to strangers, whether congenial or not, to do good-natured things in season and out of season, in fine, to render life easy to themselves and their neighbours under any circumstances.

We were excessively amused by one young lieutenant fresh from St. Cyr, who told us that he hoped to be sent to Senegal, or to Cochin China, or to Mexico, ere long, he didn't in the least mind which of the three. "*À vrai dire!*" he added emphatically, "*j'adore l'inconnu!*"

The young gentleman who adored the Unknown, in company with his superior officers, carried us off to the Theatre in great glee. The men of our party were persuaded to dance, whilst we ladies looked on from a box. The Theatre was prettily decorated with flowers and banners, the upper ten thousand dancing on the stage, the multitude on the parterre or pit.

All classes of the little community of Milianah were here represented. There was the general's wife in satin and lace, and the general's cook in calico, stiff with starch. There were Jews, Arabs, and Kabyles among the spectators; and whilst the dancing went on merrily, some strange things might be seen in the lower boxes. The Arabs are arrant gamblers, though Mahomet particularly reprobates games of chance in the Koran, cap. v., when he says: "O believers, wine, games of chance, statues, and fortune-telling, are an abomination invented by Satan. Abstain from them and you will be happy."

But despite the command of the Prophet, play, and high play too, is still common among the faithful. Some high play was going on to-night in dark corners of this little Milianah Theatre between one or two French officers and as many dozens of Arab Aghas and Bach-Aghas. The Frenchmen held the cards, and the Arabs held, or rather tried to hold, their money, but somehow the game seemed to go against them, and the supreme indifference of the Frenchmen's manner was not to be forgotten. They really seemed to look upon the Arabs as dogs.

When, a little before midnight, we returned to the Hotel, it presented the appearance of an encampment. Beds were made up on the floors of the *salons*, and whichever way we looked, we saw some rough head resting on an improvised pillow.

Early next morning we were on our way again. The horses were fresh, the weather was perfect, and we drove briskly through a magnificent country, whose features changed at every turn of the road. Sometimes we saw Arabs at work on well-cultivated slopes and valleys, whilst at others not a soul was in sight, and not a human element seemed ever to have modified the solitudes around us.

Looking back we had a superb view of Milianah, which, from a great distance, might be compared to a white dove resting midway between heaven and earth. Above its glistening walls rose the superb peak of the Zakkar; around stretched mountain after mountain of varied aspect, whilst, at the foot of the town, lay a fertile plateau, through which we were journeying.

The road was excellent, and our Arab drivers smoked their paper cigarettes in silent satisfaction with the prospect of things. But by the time we had lost sight of Milianah, we had lost our road too, for the new military road to Teniet-el-Haad is only a thing of yesterday and not near completion. Just where the new way ended and the old began, was an encampment of about forty soldiers, whose tents, horses, and uniforms, made a bright and cheerful picture in the solitude. The sous-officier, after a little shyness, invited us to breakfast in his tent, and soon quite a feast was spread before us. Nothing could equal the hospitality and heartiness of our host, though his guests were all foreigners and strangers to him. After having wished the gentlemen plenty of sport and the ladies plenty of sketching at Teniet, he bade us adieu regretfully.

An hour or two later we reached the solitary caravansary of Anseur-el-Louzi, where we halted for the night. As we drove under the gateway, two or three dogs rushed out to try and bite us, and the little family of the caravansary came forward with a word of welcome.

They were rather rough-looking Alsatians, but well-meaning in the main, and seemed anxious to make us comfortable. The house-wife led us to the only rooms at her disposal for the

ladies, promising the gentlemen a room somewhere, and all of us a vegetable soup and roast
quails for dinner. Our rooms were those
usually set apart for the officers, who were
warned, by a printed notice stuck on the walls,
not to carry their dogs indoors with them;
the outer one opened on to the court by a
door of tremendous thickness, and the inner
looked towards the hills and the road winding
amid them by which we had come.

The caravansary was built square with
small towers at each corner for defence, and
thick walls divided into rooms and stables, all
opening upon the court, which measured about
a hundred feet by sixty. In the centre was a
large fountain, and when we arrived, a group
of Spahis in scarlet burnouses were giving
their horses drink, and chatting gravely in the
sun.

Nothing could equal the solitariness or
the Eastern aspect of the scene. The court
with its white walls cut sharply against a
burning blue sky, the fountain, the dark brown
mountaineers who came and went, the drinking camels, the meadows of asphodel and
oleanders, and the ever-changing hills beyond

—all this was not to be seen for the first time and easily forgotten.

The outlying country was lovely beyond description. We went out to pluck wild-flowers, and in ten minutes our hands were full; there were crimson anemones, the pale asphodel, the iris, white and purple, marigolds large as roses, and golden as ripe oranges, vetches purple, blue, and pink, rosemary, mignonette, and an infinity whose names I do not know. With this glory of colour on the hills, a river rippling amid oleanders below, a fresh spring air quickening our pulses, and a horizon of mountains on every side, here of the deepest green, there of dreamiest violet—who would not envy us such a walk!

One gets no twilight in Africa. The sun goes down and the stars come out in the same indescribable, delicious, tranquillising light, that is hardly of day or of night, but more beautiful than either. In a moment, as if by a miracle, the flowers at our feet are no longer cusps of glowing colour, the olive-trees lose their soft gradations of hue and shape, the sea becomes of a uniform sleepy blue, and the sky overhead is purply black and studded with stars. So it was at the caravansary, but instead of stars came rain and darkness, and we heard between our dreams the plashing drops and the jackals' cries together.

Chapter 9.

LIFE AT TENIET-EL-HAAD.— SOCIETY AT A FRENCH MILI-
TARY STATION.— A SNOW-STORM IN THE CEDAR FOREST.
—THE CEDAR FOREST ON A FINE DAY.

OLLOWING the river Chelif, that
wound amid oleanders and tamarisk
trees over a rocky bed, we pushed
on towards Teniet. The weather was still cold
and showery, and the rains of the night before
had swollen the river in many places, making
cascades and waterfalls wherever it found im-
pediment. But for the foliage I could often
have fancied myself in North Wales; there was
many a dell and rushing stream that might
have been those of Betws-y-Coed, and many
a glen and waterfall that one might find again
in Llangollen. At some places it was terrible
work to cross the jagged channel of the river,
and more than once we alighted for the horses'
sake, getting over by means of such stepping-

stones as we could find. The bright reds and greys of the rocks, the bold shapes they some-times showed against the sky, the mingled leafage of tamarisk, of oleander, of ilex, of terebinth, and of locust-tree, the pale green water creaming into surf amid blocks of polished stone, made these ravines beautiful, especially when the sun came out, and showed us a party of red-cloaked Spahis galloping across the Sierra and a wild-looking goatherd who ex-changed *Salamalek* with us as we passed by, draped in white, and posed like a king.

At mid-day we stopped at a wretched little hut, and obtained black bread, wild boar-steaks, and what our host was pleased to call a moun-tain salad, in other words, wild endive well soaked in strong oil. When we had lunched a poor-looking Arab came up with his two wives, and loitered about, looking at us, and exchanging smiles and words with each other.

The women were not ill-looking, and one of us sketched the little party, by turns, to their infinite embarrassment and delight. They seemed too ignorant to turn upon the artist as the poorest Algerian will do, and refuse to have their portraits taken on simply religious grounds; but took their turns with childish amusement and self-consciousness. We gave each half a franc for the sitting, but the husband was so enchanted at the idea of his portrait travelling to England " beyond sea," that he presented the artist with a handful of new-laid eggs out of sheer gratitude!

In Algiers no one will sit for you unless driven to it by direst need of bread, whilst no sooner do you begin to take a portrait chance-wise, than you are compelled to shut your book and put up your pencils. It is only at the extreme poles of society that any tolerance can be found. The better class of Moors have become so far infused with French culture as to patronize photography, and the Arabs of the country are too ignorant of the accepted veto in the Koran to see any harm in a portrait.

Late in the afternoon we drove through the gate of Teniet-el-Haad, to find snow on the mountains around us, snow half melted on the roadways, and a sharp north wind cutting our faces like a sword.

It was our intention to settle ourselves for several days at this little military station, and accordingly we unpacked our valises, brought

out our small supply of books, and tried to
make the best of our wretched inn. There
was no sort of accommodation for us beyond a
couple of bedrooms crowded to the last inch
with furniture, clothes, provisions, and dirt;
and looking on one side, over the barracks to
the mountains, on the other over a miserable
Arab village, and a little Catholic church
flanked by green hills sprinkled with snow.
These rooms were separated from the other
part of the house by a wooden ladder, sloppy
with snow and guarded by a vicious dog which
barked incessantly; and as we had our meals
below, we furnished ourselves with wooden
shoes for the transit. The one element of delight and comfort was a fire of huge cedar-logs
in our front room, round which we gathered,
hardly knowing which to praise most, the grateful warmth or the delicious smell of the blazing
cedar-wood. In the evening the commanding
officers to whom we had letters of introduction
came to see us. M. le Colonel was a quiet,
soldierly-looking man of about fifty, who has
seen some sharp fighting in Algeria. M. le
Capitaine, who had a young wife and some
charming children, was a burly old soldier who

had seen hard service, too, and with him came a boyish young officer of rather aristocratic appearance fresh from St. Cyr.

These gentlemen promised us horses, mules, and guides for our excursion to the cedar forest next day, and a gazelle-hunt afterwards if we only stayed for better weather.

By seven o'clock next morning we were up and looking at the weather. It was not promising. Heavy clouds half hid the mountains, and as the villagers turned out to church, umbrellas were held up one by one. We could hardly see the snow, it was so fine, but the fact could not be disputed, of snow falling and likely to fall.

The gentlemen were true to their word however, and taking that as a prognostication of good weather, we mounted the horses they had provided for us. Such a cavalcade as we formed was evidently an uncommon sight at Teniot. Jews, Arabs, and French, came out to stare at us, and by the time we were fairly started, quite a crowd had collected in the street.

Our guide led the way bearing provisions in saddle-bags. He was a handsome Kabyle.

and his soldier's dress of crimson leather leg-
gings, scarlet burnous, and white linen head-
gear, became him well.   As he moved on in
the wintry landscape before us, the warm colour
of his dress seemed especially grateful to the
eyes.   I think it is Leigh Hunt who says,
" I never see an old woman wearing a scarlet
cloak in wet weather without blessing her."
And I agree with him, that if bright tints are
acceptable in a sunny atmosphere, they are
doubly so in a wintry one.

After steadily mounting for an hour and a
half we entered upon the skirts of the cedar
forest.   Here we saw two or three solitary
Arab tents.   As we ascended we gained a
wider and yet a wider view of the surrounding
country, till at last we reached a summit from
which even Milianah was visible.   But the
sky was overcast, the snow began to fall without intermission, and very soon we could only
see the immediate scenery around us.   Never
shall I forget the grandeur of the cedar forest
as we saw it in a snow-storm.   At first we
had no words for our admiration of those
kingly cedars, which seemed to have sent out
their gigantic branches in the throes of some

K

superhuman struggle with an infinite power, and now stood like towers of strength, clothed in plumes of glossy green. The height of the trees, the size of the trunks, the vastness of their spreading shade, the isolation of their positions, all combine to render a forest of cedars supreme and superb in effect. But when the mist came rolling down the mountains, and the storm-wind wrapt the stately crests in snow, the scene was unparalleled.

Far as the eye could reach, stretched an abysmal prospect of grey mist, from which rose here and there a monster tree, whose dark branches took a spectral look in the surrounding solitude. Indeed, so superhuman was the solitude that one almost looked for a megatherium or megalonyx to break it, and no lesser or later created living thing. One felt, too, that some realisation of annihilation was possible in sight of this infinite desolation and silence hitherto unpreconceived. The wail of Ossian, the story of Prometheus, and the music of Beethoven, may perhaps be compared to such a scene, but only the Promethean legend equals it in solemn majesty. Every one of those Titanic trunks looked as if it might have been forced to the verge of the abyss in some half-godlike, half-human struggle with a higher power; and the wind, as it swept down from the mountains, groaned and gasped out an expression of positive pain. One longs to be a poet under such inspirations.

We followed a wild tract that led, now on the verge of an awful precipice, now through the mazes of the forest, and at last reached a deserted hut standing on a little plateau. Blackened stems, just silvered with snow, lay here and there, whilst our point of sight was bounded by trees in their full prime and glory, some of them reaching to the height of twenty yards, and capable of sheltering a hundred and twenty mounted soldiers from the sun.

We had hoped to make a little fire in the hut for the purpose of drying our soaked clothes and warming our benumbed limbs, but, unfortunately, neither the guide nor our cavaliers were provided with lucifers. There was nothing to do but to make ourselves happy. Our saddle-bags were produced, and we made a hearty meal standing on boards, and shifting from one foot to the other by way of keeping up circulation. When our supply of hard-boiled eggs, bread, and wine had come to an end, the storm had gathered in force and fury. Down came the artillery of winds, crashing, laming, ruining wherever they passed, and gloating over destruction with shrieks and yells of triumph. Fast and thick came the rattling charge of snow-flakes, covering every speck of greenness and every sign of life till the eye became dazzled with the glistering monotony. To go on was madness, to remain was a madness worse still; so we remounted and faced the storm with as much courage and good humour as we had at command. For some time we kept in a path that wound through the very heart of the forest, having a steep ravine on each side, and gaining at every turn a new prospect of wild and weird effect. The mist was now so thick that the huge cedars looked diaphanous and visionary seen through such a medium.

We seemed to be wandering through an atmosphere that was wholly new, peopled by pale blue phantoms of antediluvian size and mystery. As soon as we began to descend, the poor horses and mules had much ado to keep their footing, and at last some of us were obliged to dismount and walk the rest of the way out of regard for their necks and our own. Wet to the skin, our cheeks tingling from the effects of snow and wind, our limbs aching with cold, we reached Teniet as it was growing dusk, a little indisposed to accept the kind hospitality tendered to us. For the Captain insisted upon carrying us off to his pretty Moorish house to dinner, and nothing could exceed the good-nature with which he waited whilst our dresses were dried in an oven close by, and such toilettes were made as were possible to us. We found the Captain's family charming; his wife, young, pretty, and a very model of a hostess—his children full of friendliness to us—himself genial and cosmopolitan in his views regarding most things.

The only drawback to the enjoyment of the pretty dinner they had provided for us, was an accident that happened at the onset. We were just seated at table, and Hamet, the Kabyle servant, was bringing in the soup when by some inadvertent piece of awkwardness, the tureen tipped over, to the marring of the spotless damask, the shining glass, and Madame's silk dress. But with a good-tempered shrug of the shoulders, and merely the remark, "Il faut passer de notre potage alors," our host and hostess submitted to the mischance, and all went on smoothly. The unfortunate Hamet showed no sort of awkwardness, but went on with his duties like a hero who could support an evil accident.

We saw a good deal of the Captain and his family while at Teniet, and but for them should have found our long evenings and snow-bound days somewhat dull. For the snow having set in seemed disposed to stay, and there was nothing to do but pile up our cedar-logs, bring out our books and pencils, and wait for finer weather. There was no possibility of return to Milianah even till a change came.

We picked up one or two pleasant acquaintances whilst breakfasting in the untidy little *salle-à-manger* of our inn; an intelligent Maronite interpreter, who presented me with a copy of the Testament in Arabic, and offered to give me lessons during my stay; a couple of intelligent lads, who also spoke Arabic very well, and brought us their grammars to look at, and several others who gave us information and interchanged civilities at every opportunity. Madame B——'s Arab servant brought in a little wild boar one day which some one had offered to him for a few francs, and we carried the little creature home to Algiers, where it still fattens and flourishes. This Arab servant was a boy of fifteen, who had never been away from Algiers before, and looked upon Teniet as the great world, which, having once seen, people are wise.

"Well, Hamet," I said, "isn't it a pleasant thing to run about the world a bit and see how other people live?"

"Ma foi, oui, Madame," he answered, scratching his head ruefully, "c'est un très bonne chose de voyager, mais je serai très content, moi, de revoir Alger. On se trouve fou quand on ne connait personne."

Hamet was an excellent lad, devoted to his mistress, obliging to us, honest, active, and thoughtful for our comfort, but he lacked the art of looking cheerful under adverse circum-

stances. Ill content with the cold, the want
of his usual occupations, and the absence of
his fellow-servants, he lounged about the door
of the inn smoking paper cigarettes, and looking the very picture of melancholy.

Madame R——, the wife of the Captain,
was with us a good deal, and when the men
were out riding despite the bad weather, we
ladies amused ourselves indoors.   It was a
very pretty picture of domestic life that we saw
at the little military station of Teniet-el-Haad.
Madame R—— was a perfect housekeeper.
She taught her children, she made their clothes,
she supervised the business of the kitchen, she
presided over her table, and she entertained
her guests with a grace and ease perfectly
charming.   She was accomplished too, sang
and played exceedingly well, could discuss the
best of our English authors intelligently, and
knew a great deal about the country in which
she lived.   Her account of her African experience was touching in the extreme.   She had
come out from France as a young bride of
eighteen, and till within the last year or two,
had constantly suffered anxiety on her hus-

band's account. Sometimes he had been sent
into the interior, sometimes he had been sub-
duing Arab or Kabyle tribes within a day's
journey from her, and more than once she had
been in imminent peril of her life.

"Here at Teniet last year," she said, "just
before my baby was born, we were in a state
of awful fear. A caravansary not far from
here had been surprised by Arabs in the night,
the door set fire to, the people murdered, and
unmentionable horrors perpetrated. My husband was fighting a tribe of insurgents some
way off in the mountains, and we had only
a few soldiers left in the fort; for nights and
nights, I and the two ladies who were here
with me were kept awake by apprehension for
ourselves and our husbands. Now, thank
God, all is quiet immediately around us, but
no one knows how long it will be so."

One evening we were invited to a dinner-
party at the Caserne, given by the Colonel.
His bachelor rooms were very pretty, and en-
livened by the presence of a tame gazelle,
which played an infinity of tricks. The walls
were decorated with very beautiful skins of

panthers, hyenas, gazelles, and jackals, most of which he had himself taken in the hunt; and also with Kabyle arms and Moorish carpets, spoils of many a skirmish in the interior.

At last the weather broke, and as if by enchantment, all was golden sunshine and greenness. We went into the cedar forest hardly believing our eyes. Soft breaths of wild flowers were blown across our faces; the tips of the cedar boughs were burnished with tender light; pleasant sounds of trickling water came to our ears as we passed on; the mountains stood out in the sunny atmosphere like gems in clear water; all was freshness, and softness, and beauty.

We made a pic-nic in a lovely spot, and lingered there for hours well content. Before us, the high lands of the forest parted, showing a stupendous peak crowned by a solitary cedar, and a vast prospect of hill and valley mellowed and softened by the genial sunlight. The knoll on which we bivouacked was a very paradise of verdure, and on each side dipped sheer into intricate mountain ways and thickets. Panthers make their haunts in these solitudes,

and we had been expressly enjoined not to
linger within the precincts of the forest after
four o'clock; but it was a hard restriction to
put upon lovers of sunsets and evening skies.
However, we had no wish to see any panthers,
and returned home just as the sun was redden-
ing the vast plain of the Little Desert below
Teniet, and the cedar forest was growing weird
and awful again.

One sees the cedar logs blazing on the
hearths of Teniet regretfully, and with longings
to bring some home to be carved into caskets
and cabinets. This exquisite wood was one of
the dearest luxuries during the last years of
the Roman Republic. Pliny says how " the at-
traction of ivory and cedar-wood has caused us
to strip all the forests of Libya." Prefects and
proconsuls set an example of devastation which
has been followed by French commanders.
Tables of cedar-wood fetched fabulous prices
among millionnaires and connoisseurs at Rome.
Cicero bought a table for the enormous sum of
four thousand pounds, and others fetched the
prices of a fine estate. The most esteemed
were those carved from a single block, sur-
mounted on an ivory pillar and ornamented

with a circular band of gold. But what a different aspect did the forests of the Atlas present then ! Dr. Bodichon, in his *Études sur l'Algérie et l'Afrique*, shows in an interesting chapter how the Roman colonisation modified the condition, and by the demolition of forests, indeed, the climate, of North Africa. The solitary lion and panther captured at Teniet now and then, are the remnants of a savage host, once numerous as the sands of the sea ; and without doubt, the elephant, the hippopotamus, the bear, and the wild ass roamed at large among these solitudes until disturbed by the hosts of Suetonius Paulinus and Hosidius Geta.

Chapter 10.

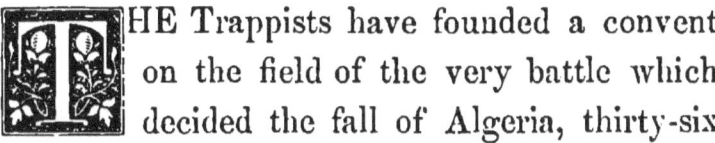

HE Trappists have founded a convent on the field of the very battle which decided the fall of Algeria, thirty-six years ago; and on a bright spring morning I joined a party of friends to visit their little colony of Staoueli.

Leaving Algiers, the road curled for a couple of hours amid homesteads of French colonists and wastes entirely uncultivated. As we ascended, the chain of the Atlas mountains seemed to rise with us, and by-and-by, we had a glorious prospect of deep blue sea, pale purple hills, whose olive-clad slopes and Moorish villas glistened against a wondrous Eastern sky. When we had left Algiers some miles behind us, we entered upon an extensive plateau, covered with the fan-like leafage of the dwarf palm, laurustinus in full blossom, clematis, wild rosemary, and other fair and fragrant children of the waste. The Trappists, however, have turned their lands into a little oasis of beauty and cultivation; and no sooner had we come within sight of their territory than we were lost in admiration of the pastures, the orchards, the vineyards, and the corn-fields of which it consisted.

The first thing that struck us as we drove up to the door of the convent was this inscription, "Les dames n'entrent pas;" and when the men of our party were carried off by an intelligent Father Superior to see the farm and *ateliers*, and the ladies were left in a dingy little parlour, with only a heavy lay-brother to entertain us, I felt inclined to rebel. A Mussulman legend came into my head, which might very well have served as an argument against these woman-hating Trappists.

All true believers, as is generally known, perhaps, have a second Koran in the so-called *Hadites*, or Conversations of Mahomet. One day, when the Prophet sat amidst a circle of young people, he explained the Word of God after this fashion,—

"Let those among you who are rich enough to support one or more wives, marry. When a man marries, the Evil One utters a terrible cry; all his angels fly to him, asking, 'What is the matter, Lord?' 'A mortal has just escaped me,' answers Satan, in despair."

Now I defy the Trappists to tell me a better story on their side than this. Mahomet also added,—

"Protect the woman; she is weak. Marry young."

Not being allowed beyond the little parlour, we tried to get all the conversation possible out of our host, the soft-voiced brother just mentioned. He, with five others, carried on the housekeeping, saw strangers, doled out benefits to the poor, and lived a little in the world. By way of entertaining us, he brought out rosaries of beads and medals all of Birmingham manufacture, tempting us to lay out a few francs in recollection of our visit to Staoueli. He next showed us a large picture adorning the wall, descanting on the merits and sanctity of the donor of it, adding, with a sigh,—

"Il faut faire quelque chose pour entrer dans le Paradis."

It didn't seem to me a very great piece of work by which Paradise was purchased, namely, the gift of a daub in oil-colours, representing the Madonna and Child; but no two people see the same rainbow! After a time he brought out a couple of devotional books, begged us to amuse ourselves with them, and went away "on hospitable thoughts intent." We found the books not quite to our taste, and preferred a stroll up and down the avenue by which we had come. The outer wall of the convent was covered with this inscription, " S'il est triste de vivre à la Trappe, qu'il est doux d'y mourir."

Well may the silence, the isolation, and the hardship of the life at Staoueli make death welcome.

When we returned, a plentiful repast of black bread, honey, fresh butter, and figs was spread before us, accompanied by wine. The melancholy *frère concierge* then retired, and one of the brothers superior entertained us. He was a shrewd, cheerful-looking man of fifty,

quite *au courant* with the affairs of the outer
world, quick to read character, and apt, I should
say, at ruling his fellow-creatures. We had
an animated discussion on the present state of
the Romish Church; and as our party consisted of a Swiss Catholic gentleman from
Berne, his Lutheran wife, a broad Churchman,
and myself, there was a diversity of opinions
to begin with.

The father beat us hollow. He was so
witty, so enthusiastic, so well-trained in the use
of facts, so apt at tripping you up with a
truism, that we had nothing to say to him,
and he saw it delightedly. Even Father Ig-
natius became a shining light, so handled; and
the Claydon affairs were made to appear sub-
ject-matter of glorious triumph to the Catholic
Church. When other subjects were brought
forward, our host had plenty to tell us about
his convent and its prospects. He seemed
pleased to hear his wine praised, which, with
everything else on the table, was the produce
of the Trappist farms, and brought out some
oranges of particular flavour as a special little
attention.

We were quite sorry to go, and promised

L

the father we should not easily forget either
our talk or our entertainment at Staoueli.
There is something else too at Staoueli that
one never forgets, and that is, a magnificent
group of palms in the courtyard. So many
palms were cut down when the French took Algiers, that a new comer cannot fail to be
disappointed at finding them so scarce. One
pictures how

> " Mid far sands
> The palmtree-cinctured city stands,
> Bright white beneath, as heaven bright blue
> Above it."

Whereas palm-trees are so scarce about Algiers, that one's heart thrills with pleasure to
see them, and instead of sands, its surroundings
are all verdant and varied hill and dale.

We came home by way of Sidi Ferruch, a
dreary spot on the coast, where the French
first landed in 1830. From thence to Algiers
our attention was chiefly directed to the French
farms, through which we passed ; poor little
colonies cropping up in the waste with a positive human look of sadness about them. Here
and there one might see a few goats and sheep

herded by an Arab boy; or a solitary horse
tethered to a bit of broken wall; or a tiny hut
that might have been Robinson Crusoe's,
around which children were playing in the sun.
The sun shone brightly on these poor little
homesteads and the green slopes around them,
but they looked desolate nevertheless. In
some places we saw some toiling colonist dig-
ging up the picturesque but pernicious dwarf-
palm; and in others, potatoes and grain had
been planted between little groups of them, as
if the task of extermination had been given up
in despair.

The last few miles of the journey from Sidi
Ferruch to Algiers remind one of the Cornish
coast. Bold rocks dip sheer into a transparent
sea of pure green; the sands are white and
shining; the waves are sometimes dashed with
tumultuous fury against their stormy barrier,
and sometimes ebb and flow so gently as scarce
to be heard at all.

This coast is full of interest. At one point
you pass a ruined Moorish fort, whose broken
towers projecting over the sea would afford
sensation novelists excellent scenes for murder.

We stopped our horses and explored these

ruins, as far as exploration was safe. Then we took coffee in a quaint, little Moorish *café*, looking upon an Arab cemetery crowded with ghost-like figures draped in white. These were Moorish women praying to their dead. It was Friday, the Mahometan Sabbath, when those who have lost husbands, fathers, or children, flock to the graveyards, and commune with the spirits of the departed. They take *kous-kous*, the national food, with them; they call on the dead to eat, to drink, to give counsel or comfort, and it is believed seldom come away unheard. But there is another side to the picture. These Moorish women lead rather dull lives at home, and if they don't go to the cemeteries to pray, they go just the same to see their friends and be merry. Friday is, indeed, their only holiday. Who can wonder that they use and abuse it?

Children take part in this custom, which I imagine represents little else but a piece of merry-making to them. A friend of mine, an artist, told me that she had taken a little Arab into a cemetery, where she was painting, in order to carry her things to and fro. The urchin got tired of waiting for his patroness, and after a while chose to squat himself on the very stone she was sketching.

"Don't you see that you are hindering my work?" said the lady: "get away, at once!"

"I must be here; I'm praying to the bones of my father," answered the child, with perfect *nonchalance*, and my friend began to work upon another tomb on her canvas. Her little persecutor was too clever to be so hindered from his purpose, and immediately changed his position, as effectually hiding the second stone as he had done the first. On being remonstrated with sharply, he replied, "I must be here; I'm praying to the bones of my grandfather."

And nothing but kicks and blows would have sent him away.

Chapter 11.

CHERCHELL.—A COLONIST FAMILY.—AN ARAB FAIR.—THE
ORCHARD OF ALMOND-TREES.—THEATRICALS.—AN ARAB
FUNERAL.

NE never grows tired of crossing the
plain of the Metidja, so famous in
Algerian story. There is an unde-
finable charm in the vastness and variety of its
brown wastes and sunny oases, in its interminable lines and breadths of colour, in its
unexpected villages smiling like wild flowers
amid nests of verdure, in its broken, but har-
monious masses of desert and corn-fields, of
hill and plain, of wilderness and cultivation.

The Metidja has been a battle-field in more
senses than one, for during the first years of
French occupation disease made it one huge
grave. "The colonists died like flies," as the
phrase went, of the deadly nuisance, engendered
by swamp and marsh, and not till an effective
drainage was carried out, did the mortality

cease. Even now ague is as common in the villages as marsh-fever in some parts of Sussex, though these very villages may be perfect little paradises of cultivation, ease, and plenty.

The journey from Blidah to Cherchell takes you through some very pretty and prosperous French settlements, and long as it is, offers too much matter of interest to prove tedious.

We started from Blidah at six o'clock one morning in an open car. The day was just breaking, and in spite of cloaks and shawls, it was very cold till the sun came out. For the first few miles the road lay as straight as a line could be drawn through well-cultivated vineyards and fields of corn, of cotton, of tobacco, and of flax, and trim villages, that might make one believe oneself to be in France. The country was rich, and though the rivers were all but dry, there were little springs at each village, and plenty of water everywhere. Wild irises, purple and white, grew plentifully by the wayside, also the familiar daisy wild mignonette and rosemary. Olives and carob-trees made a pleasant shelter now and then, and the fields were divided by hedges of aloe and Barbary fig. Now and then, we met

a farmer driving himself to market in a rude
gig or cart, or a troop of Arabs and negroes
driving cattle and sheep ; or we saw a wild-
looking little fellow in a ragged burnous, keeping goats or cows in the thick brushwood, or
a French or Arab farmer ploughing a tiny
field; but the scene was very solitary for the
most part.

At Marengo we stopped and breakfasted.
The landlord and landlady of the village hostelry were Germans, and on finding out that one
of my fellow-travellers was of the same nation,
no words could sufficiently express their welcome.   The eldest daughter of the house was
a very Gretchen in prettiness and innocence,
and for her sake especially we got interested
in the family.   They had come from North
Germany, and did not seem at all discontented
with their prospects, though they declared any
idea of saving money to be quite out of the
question.

"We can maintain our family of seven
children respectably, but that is all," they said,
"and we shall never see the dear Fatherland
again, never—never!"

"And the Arabs," we said, "how do you

get on with them? Naturally you have much to do with each other!"

"The dear God, yes! we have plenty to do with them, and can't say that they are worse than Christians. Perhaps, here and there, one will have two wives or will steal your poultry. But does no one steal poultry, or do worse than marry two wives, in Europe? That's what we should like to know!"

The children, who could hardly speak a word of French, took us by the hand to see the church and the village. It happened to be market-day, and we saw a busy and picturesque scene that we had not looked for.

In a large field bordered by carob-trees were some hundreds of Arabs and Kabyles, some squatted beneath the shade, others were grouped around a horse or a score of sheep, others wandered about, like ourselves, content to be spectators only.

We saw some faces of marvellous wildness and character; of beauty, too, though beauty to us of such unaccustomed kind, that, at first, it seemed positive ugliness. So used as we Europeans are to a uniform trimness of exterior and neatness of type, we cannot for a long time realize the charm of perfectly untrained and unconventional symmetry of form and feature. There were limbs and lineaments here that realized all one's pre-conceived ideas of patriarchal times. These brown-cheeked, stalwart sons of Ishmael might well have figured in the life-stories that were fierce and isolated as their own deserts; and as we lingered about the market, we saw many a Nebajoth bartering for corn or cattle.

We were witness, too, of more than one little scene of Biblical pathos and simplicity. Whilst engaged in talking to a very well-dressed, handsome young fellow, who could speak a little French, a white-bearded, venerable, but ragged, old man came up and greeted him by name. In the twinkling of an eye our companion had excused himself gracefully for quitting us so hastily, and had fallen on his friend's neck, and kissed him. Then they drew aside and chatted together. And this sort of scene we saw repeated more than once.

There were a few Kabyles with their wives at the fair; some of whom were eating figs and talking volubly under the shade. The men, with their greasy leathern aprons, coarse shirts,

and bare cropped heads, contrast greatly to
their own disadvantage with the Arabs, who
always look clean and gentlemanly under any
circumstances.

Leaving Marengo, we soon entered into
a wilder district, ever having before us a beautifully shaped mountain of pale transparent
blue. On either side stretched wastes of brushwood and dwarf-palm, solitary as death, save
for the rare smoke of a settler's chimney, or
the cry of a goatherd among the thickets.
The sky was fickle, but brilliant, and as we
drove along, we had superb aspects of distant
mountains and surrounding plain.

Near Cherchell the scenery became magnificent. Now we dipped into the heart of a
smiling gold green valley: now we traversed
the edge of a gloomy ravine; now we crossed
a dry river-bed, overhung by the tasseled
tamarisk and the glossy Aleppo pine ; or we
threaded an olive-grove through which the sun
could but sparsely penetrate.

A cry of admiration escaped our lips as a
turn of the road brought us in sight of a wide
spreading valley, crossed at the base by a
superb Roman aqueduct. Perfect, but for one

arch, and standing in the midst of fertile fields, this structure impresses one with an unspeakable feeling of pleasurable surprise. One thinks so much of the Arabs and Kabyles in Algeria, that one forgets what a part the Romans first played there till reminded of it in this way.

Nothing can be prettier or more poetic than the view of Cherchell, as approached from the land side. Its white walls form an amphitheatre, above which rise green hills and fragrant gardens, whilst below, the bright blue sea extends as far as the eye can reach. At this time of the year the almond-tree was in full flower; and I cannot describe the effect of the pure pink blossoms that flushed the hills like a rosy cloud. These brilliant colours, the enamel of the turf, the pale yellow of the seashore, the soft, deep turquoise of the waves, the rosy hue of the almond-tree, the glistening white of the mosques and roofs, seemed so near the eyes that one rubbed them, feeling but just awaked from the blindness of partial sleep. I can still shut my eyes and revel in the night picture of Cherchell as it looked on that summer day. For though we were only in March the weather was that of summer-time.

A little Arab volunteered to show us the Roman ruins, but did not in the least know where they were, and but for a stern Maltese, who sent him off with a cuff and a scolding, we might have wandered about in vain for hours. The Maltese, having given vent to his indignation, proved no sort of a guide himself, so we trusted to our own eyes, which was, after all, the safest plan. After wandering about a little hither and thither, we needed no history to tell us of the ancient glory of Cherchell, the Iol of the Carthaginians and the Julia Cæsarea of the Romans.

These broken columns and capitals, these disinterred statues and frescoes, these monumental stones and sculptured altars, tell their own story—a story of barbaric pomp, of Roman conquest, of proconsular power, of Christian martyrdom, of fluctuating triumphs and falls without number. One reads the history of Cherchell palimpsest-wise from these records. The Phœnician story comes first, then the Roman, then the Vandal, then the Turkish; but the first are clearest and most interesting.

The most remarkable monuments at Cherchell are those of the Hippodrome, the circus where

Saint Severin and his wife, St. Aquila, were burned alive, and the Thermæ. But on a verdant slope stretching to the sea and shaded by chestnut-trees, are heaps of later discovered treasures, such as columns, cornices, and friezes, which are no less interesting, and amongst these we wandered for upwards of an hour. Day was over; Arabs, Kabyles, French, and Spaniards (for there are great numbers of Spaniards in these little colonies), were walking about, or chatting as they sat on some fragment of sculptured stone; a fresh breeze blew from the sea, and the whole scene was one of peace and pleasantness.

The smaller treasures discovered at Cherchell are collected in a little museum, and the greater part of them are exhibited in a tiny garden opening on to the street. Here we saw a faun, terribly disfigured by time and accident, but sunny and beaming with life nevertheless; a graceful Diana; delicately carved capitals, busts, monumental stones, cinerary urns, amphoræ, and other waifs and strays saved from the wreck of the once flourishing Mauritanian capital.

One of the most curious things is an altar

set up by a Roman prætor to the Mauritanian gods.

Leaving the museum we started through the town under the escort of an intelligent young soldier, an Alsatian, who, seeing that we were strangers, offered his services. He took us first, naturally enough, to the barracks, and showed us the little theatre which had been constructed by himself and fellow-men, and was patronised by the officers and residents of the town.

Outside the doors was pasted a bill bearing the following notice in a bold hand:—

TO-NIGHT WILL BE GIVEN,

MADELEINE,

A VAUDEVILLE IN THREE ACTS BY
M. LE CAPITAINE TARVER.

——

Doors open at seven o'clock.   Admission free.

"Do come and see us play," said our guide, persuasively. "M. le Capitaine writes such pretty pieces, and M. le Sous-lieutenant is to play the part of Madeleine. I assure you, ladies and gentlemen, that but for our theatre we should die of *ennui* in this out-of-the-way spot."

We excused ourselves from accepting his kind invitation, as we intended to leave Cherchell the next day, and were anxious to see as much of it as possible. He took alike the refusal and apology good-temperedly, and strolled with us to the Christian burial-ground, which covered a lovely hill-side reaching to the sea.

"Ah!" mused our companion with a sigh: "it's a pity to give us such a large cemetery at Cherchell, where it's so healthy that we positively never die!"

"Is it in truth so healthy?" I asked.

"So healthy that people never die except of old age, Madame. How can it be otherwise with the sea on one side, and dry, warm hills on the other? We never suffer from heat or cold, or ague or fever: and though the life is a little monotonous here, there are many things to enjoy."

Whilst we were loitering among the graves, reading a name here, plucking a dead rose

there, we saw a strange procession hastening
down a hill-side opposite to us. It was an
Arab funeral. The body, wrapped in a wretched
cerecloth of thin woollen stuff, was borne on
the shoulders of four men who led the way,
the mourners and tribe following. As they
went, they chanted verses from the Koran; and
the weird wail of the chant and the wild figures
of the men as they bore towards us, treading
down the sweet asphodels in their haste, and
bearing bunches of prickly cactus in their hands,
made a strange picture.

There was one poor mourner who separated
himself from the crowd in his great grief, and
tottered and trembled like one drunken, whilst
he gave utterance to such moans as one hears
from poor beasts robbed of their cubs. It was
pitiful to hear.

They walked so quickly that it was with
much ado we could keep up to them, but in a
quarter of an hour we had reached a solitary
burial-ground overlooking the sea.

And the body was placed into a shallow
grave, with neither coffin nor shroud, the face
turned towards Mecca, the marabout repeated

M

the prayer for the dead, the grave was heaped up with stones and faggots to protect it from the jackals, and all was over.

The solitariness of the cemetery, the savage simplicity of the rites, the wild, yet sorrowful, faces of the crowd, made the whole scene strik- ing, but not so striking as one we saw early next day.

It was Friday, the Mussulman sabbath, and when we visited the new-made grave, we found it covered with branches of olive, of ilex, and of uprooted aloe, whilst a group of female mourners were squatted round it, chanting the virtues of the dead.

There was something in their white figures and monotonous wail, whilst perhaps the lines of smoke rising from the little valley below reminded them of souls fleeing upward; and the broad blue sea beyond, of the happy eternity for which they were praying.

I am not sure whether the prayers for the dead around Algiers are precisely those in use among the tribes of the Desert, which are sin- gularly touching and beautiful. The ceremony is almost the same, only more imposing. If the deceased be a chief, his horse is led in the procession by a slave, his gun, his yataghan and his spurs are suspended from his saddle. A number of hired female mourners chant lamentations, and all the tribe follow their dead lord to his grave, joining in the burden of the marabout's prayer, " There is but one God ; and Mahomet is the Prophet of God."

Chapter 12.

LIFE IN THE COUNTRY.—A TURK SPEAKS HIS MIND.—A
PIC-NIC IN AFRICA. —TWILIGHT. —THE PENITENTIARY
OF LA MAISON CARRÉE.—A MOORISH PALACE.

THE last days of March and the opening
ones of April I spent at the house of
a friend on the lovely heights of Mustapha Supérieure. The weather was uniformly
brilliant : we had pic-nics, a carnival, a tour-
nament, a mask ball at the theatre, and in fine,
matters of interest and amusement without end.
But before describing these things I must say
a word about our life among the hills and all
the surroundings by which it was made so
delightful.

The house overlooks Algiers and the sea.
We go to sleep with the singing of the waves
in our ears and wake to see glorious flashes
of sunrise on the fairy-like city with its white

mosques, and the green hills sloping to a glistening shore.

From the terrace of the garden, a steep path shaded by agave and wild cactus, leads to the village, and often and often have I followed it to catch the early omnibus for Algiers. If too early, it was pleasant to stroll into the pretty Moorish house at the foot of the hill, which has been turned into a church for Catholic worship. If too late, there was no other alternative but that of walking into the town. No unpleasant one, truly, for the road wound amid steep hill‑sides clothed with fragrant trees, the orange, the almond, and the fig, now first shedding its waxy, bright green leaves.

There was always plenty to do in Algiers; lessons in Arabic ; visits to the Moorish schools ; searches in the publishers' shops for new books and pamphlets; for photographs in the numerous photographic *ateliers;* calls of ceremony, and talks and purchases in the bazaars. One gets quite a circle of acquaintances among the native merchants, and as they do not economise time after our fashion, but live in one long protracted state of

leisure, the longer you dawdle over your purchases the better. Some of these men are
particularly well-mannered, intelligent, and
obliging; impoliteness one never meets with,
and the politeness of good nature is very common. They will tell you when any Mussulman
fête is to take place; will put themselves out
of the way to obtain information of Aïssaoua
dances, or Negro sacrifices, or Moorish wed-
dings; will send you an escort, and will prove
useful in a hundred and fifty ways to civil
customers. Sometimes tourists (though I am
happy to say that I have never seen my own
countrymen offend in this way) will inter-
lard their conversation with such speeches as
these, " Tell me now, *entre nous,* how many
wives have you ?" or, " How do you manage
to keep the peace between your wives ?" without remembering, or caring to remember, how
even amongst their most intimate friends the
Arabs do not mention their women. Instead
of our hearty " How d'ye do, Brown; hot day;
how's your wife and the youngsters ?" they
make their greeting after this round-about,
but dignified fashion, " May your day be happy!
Is it well with your tent ? Is it well with your

family? Is it well with your people? Is it well with your grandmother?"

And this seeming squeamishness of etiquette where women are concerned does not proceed from jealousy alone, but from a feeling of deference to the sex. A well-bred Arab never accustoms himself to " tutoyer" the mother of his children, but always addresses her in the second person.

I shall not forget how often I was scandalised by the indelicacy of a very good-tempered Swiss, the husband of an acquaintance of mine, who never entered a bazaar without blundering head-foremost into a very quagmire of ill-breeding. He would ask in a breath, " How many wives have you? which do you love best? how do they like each other?" and a dozen similar questions, all of which would be gently turned off in this way, " Oh, monsieur, I am a poor devil, and can hardly afford to keep myself!" or, " Monsieur, we only marry one wife ;" or, if the speaker were a wag, "Monsieur, I have three wives, and I love the ugliest best, because she leads me a quiet life."

Generally speaking, the men so addressed would look humiliated, and I felt no little shame myself at witnessing such offences against good taste. The Swiss saw neither the one nor the other, nor could the looks and nudges of his wife deter him from his inquiries.

There was a stout, rather conceited, but very obliging Turk, with whom I had many a long chat, when looking over his treasures of silks, of amber, and of jewels. One day he shut his door and unbosomed himself about the French. "The French here are a set of scoundrels," he said, "and no good can ever come of them. Before the French conquest I was too rich, and now I do tolerably well, but I make no money. You English are liked well enough, but then you only come for a time ; if you settled in Algiers, we should have something to be glad about. After all the fine talk when the Emperor had gone, what came of it ? And now it is not we who are to get anything, but the Kabyles, a set of dirty savages, who live like animals, and eat acorns like the pigs. Faugh! Kabyles, indeed, good luck to those who try to civilise them."

It is not to be expected that French, Turks, Arabs, and Kabyles should entertain brotherly love for each other, but one gets a little startled by such explosions of personal feeling at first. This worthy Turk had doubtless the best of reasons for regarding the conquest so bitterly; but I question whether any Arab or Kabyle holding the same opinion, could be found. He was very charitable, and often to the very scape-goats he abused so heartily; for more than once I found a ragged Arab or Kabyle sitting at his door, of whom he would in an undertone say, "Here is a poor man, the father of many children, to whom I have just given a dinner. If Madame wants a porter for her purchases, let her employ this poor man, who will thankfully earn a sou."

Sometimes he would be surrounded by his friends, drinking coffee and smoking, when I invariably went away, promising to look in some other time. There was never any obsequious apology or solicitation of custom, but a grave salute and majestic wave of the hand only. I think one must come to Algiers to learn the art of transacting business leisurely, and unlearning awkwardness of any kind. Does the pleasant influence of sunshine make good breeding so easy? I daresay, since good temper is the secret of it,—and who can help

being good-tempered where there are no clouds
or fogs ?

No less pleasant than these mornings in
town were the afternoon drives and walks.
By two o'clock the carriage would be at the
door,—horses and carriage trim as only French
grooms can make them,—and whichever way
we went, we found landscapes of beauty past
describing. One day we had a pic-nic,—and
such a pic-nic !

About four miles from Mustapha Supérieure
is a pretty Arab village, called La Bouzarea,
and thither we went one lovely afternoon in
March. We were a party of twenty in all,
and nothing could be more delightful than the
quick drive through the open country, now
brilliant with wild flowers of every character
and colour. Arrived at La Bouzarea, we
alighted at the little French hostelry in the
new village, and took a winding foot-path that
led to a quaint Arab cemetery, and an Arab
village, and panoramic view of the surrounding
country.

Though it was now five o'clock, it was too
warm to ramble about, so shawls and cushions
were spread on the knoll of rising ground, and

we feasted off tea, cakes, and strawberries, beneath the shadow of the olive-trees. Now and then, we caught glimpses of eager little brown faces peering above through the branches; and when we had done, a score of urchins in tattered burnouses gathered round the remains of the feast, one receiving an orange, another a cake, a third a banana, all scuttling about in their glee, like eager young animals at feeding-time.

We first strolled through the cemetery, a lovely spot, shaded by clusters of the dwarf-palm, and having in the midst a little koubba or tomb of a saint, built like a tiny mosque, and of purest white.

The graves lay scattered around, and over some of them were raised handsome monuments, consisting mostly of an armed death's head and foot-stone connected by a coping, all richly carved. The inscriptions are always simple, and merely state how here, deceased by the will of God, lay Fatima, the daughter of Ahmed, the son of Abderrahman, the son of Hassan, and so forth.

Having a troop of little Arabs at our heels, we then visited the village, a collection of wretched mud hovels, from which issued wild-

looking women and girls, with dark locks hanging about their cheeks, and dressed in loose
garments of sacking bound round the waist by
a woollen girdle and bare brown feet.

All smiled at us, and one or two of the younger girls joined the juvenile rabble behind us,
grinning and gesticulating.   They looked quite
pretty despite the uncleanliness of their appearance, but with a prettiness that was of a purely
animal nature.   You felt inclined to whistle
and snap your fingers to them, as you would
to pretty little dogs.

From this little Arab colony, the view is
superb and of immense extent.   The eye ranges
over sea and city, plain and rock, hill and
valley, till it is tired with so much exertion,
and rests with a feeling of positive refreshment,
on the green undulations of La Bouzarea.

We sat down on a slope of turf, looking
across a deep valley and an extent of diversi-
fied country to the bold coast of Sidi Ferruch.
It was now evening, and just as the sun set,
a wondrous mist rolled upwards from the sea.
At once, as if under the spell of some divine
enchantment, the colour died out of the waves,
the rocks grew pale and phantom-like, the trees

looked mere shadows seen in this weird atmosphere. Nothing stood out sharp and clear save some monster reeds that fringed the mountain-path below us, and these so golden in the sunshine, so delicate when pencilled against a blue sky, waved to and fro like gigantic black feathers of some antediluvian birds.

When we left La Bouzarea, all was growing clear and bright, and natural again, and we drove home in that delicious light, half of day, half of night, that we Northerners do not dream of. In England twilight is beautiful, but we see nothing, and the shadows and masses of subdued colour and perfumes of unseen flowers, are enchanting only from the mystery attached to them. In Algiers nothing is blurred or altered. The tender outlines of Oriental foliage, the radiance of mosque and palace, the silhouette of ship and lighthouse against a silvery sea, all these lose nothing of their individuality, but only gain in tenderness and beauty when seen through this fascinating and marvellous atmosphere.

When there was no especial project in hand, we had walks, rides, and drives of unspeakable variety and interest. Five minutes' walk from the house lived a poor but respectable Arab family, and often and often we walked across the fields to visit them. At a first glimpse of us the little ones would scamper within, but the elder children were not so shy, and trotted alongside of us to the house, speaking all the French they knew. There were three or four little girls much of an age, who looked wondrously pretty and picturesque in their saucy Fez caps, and full cotton trousers of pink or yellow. They had a trick of dressing themselves with chains of wild-flowers, and one can hardly give an idea of their brilliant gipsydom then; the yellow marigolds and scarlet berries seemed positively to shine with a lustre on their rich brown skins. These wild little things, named respectively Zorah, Fatima, Hanyfa, and Ayesha, all sat to my friend by turns, but proved as intractable as young colts. They would never come unless driven to it by hunger, and when tired of the business would make grimaces and contort themselves like earwigs under a glass. Still it was great good luck to get them at all, for nothing can equal the universal prejudice against sitting.

The dwelling-house of this little family was fairly comfortable, and whitewashed with scrupulosity from top to bottom. The women, there were two or three, made us very welcome, took us into all the rooms, tried to understand what we said, and to give us all the information in their power. But they hardly mustered a dozen words of French between them, and we never succeeded in learning the relationship of each to each. They only spoke of one "Baba," that is, husband, and yet seemed to live in perfect harmony. The younger of them had a little toddling boy of a year and some months old, who seemed a special pet with the girls, and they showed us a sort of hammock where he slept.

The house had three stories, and the beds were laid in stone niches in the wall. In one room hung a talisman brought from Mecca, which was evidently an object of great veneration, but of course there is no arriving at the real state or degree of religion among the women. Only a long residence in the East and a knowledge of Arabic could make that possible. The experiment must be an interesting one, and has already been tried

by Madame Luce of Algiers, the directress of
the first industrial school for Moorish girls.
This lady's endeavour to educate Moorish
women without any plan of conversion, and
indeed her whole life, form matter of most
instructive consideration and inquiry.

But I have not done with our country life
yet. One day we visited the House of Cor-
rection, or Maison Carrée, in the plain of the
Metidja. A pleasant railway journey of half-
an-hour along the sea-shore brought us to a
straggling though prosperous-looking village
dominated by a square fort. This village
might be called a martyrs' burial-ground, from
the number of victims to malaria who have
fallen there; but good drainage is doing its
work, and with care and a proper hygiène one
may now attain to the full measure of one's
days at the Maison Carrée. In former years
it was pronounced uninhabitable from November to June.

The country is wild, but verdant with hedges
of wild cacti overgrown with golden creepers,
luxuriant turf, and undulations of moor broken
here and there, showing the red earth, like a

ripe fig cut to its rosy core. We followed a winding road, having before us some Arabs riding their camels, whilst around stretched the plain, patched with oases of cultivation, and bound by the lovely outline of the Atlas mountains, looking distant and dreamy as the soft blue sky above it. The Fort has been turned into a prison within the last few years, and dreary enough is its aspect seen from the pleasant road below.

We were allowed to see over every part of the building, and found the arrangements un-exceptionable. Every place was clean, well ventilated, and not overcrowded ; the food was wholesome, the hours of work supportable; and though there was a chapel attached, every prisoner was allowed to say his prayers after his own fashion.

We saw one poor fellow performing his ablutions with dust instead of water prior to the mid-day prayer; herein following out a command of the Prophet. "If you cannot find water," says Mahomet, "rub your face and hands with fine clean sand." (Kor. v. cap. v. 9.) The cells mostly opened on to the court, and

N

on the threshold of one sat two men, one an old negro, the other an Arab, playing at some sort of game with black and white pebbles. Others were airing themselves ; but the greater number were at work in a long shed making baskets. The invalids formed a touching spectacle. They were basking in the sun in the little garden belonging to the hospital, and looked ghastly and despairing, despite of the comparative comforts with which they were indulged.

There are 600 inmates in this prison. The chief crime among the Arabs seems to be incendiarism, and next to that theft.

A far pleasanter but hardly more interesting visit, was one we paid next day to the Governor's summer palace at Mustapha Supérieure. To give an idea of this enchanting place I must quote the Laureate, how we—

> " Emerged and came upon the great
>   Pavilion of the Caliphate,
>   Right to the carven cedarn doors,
>   Flung inward over spangled floors.
>   Broad-based flights of marble stairs,
>   Ran up with golden balustrade,
>   After the fashion of the time,
>   And humour of the golden prime
>   Of good Haroun Alraschid."

The palace is entirely Moorish, and stands in gardens which may well be called "a realm of pleasure," abounding in—

> —— " Many a shady chequered lawn,
> Full of the city's stilly sound,
> And deep myrrh thickets blowing round,
> The stately cedar, tamarisks,
> Thick rosaries of scented thorn,
> Tall orient shrubs and obelisks."

Sultry as it was this April day, we found grateful shade under the orange-trees, laden alike with fruit and flower, and cool breaths of air beside fountains overhung with myrtle and oleander, and the delicate fruit and foliage of the lemon; whilst the fairy-like palace of which we caught glimpses now and then made us fancy ourselves in the golden age of Seville or Granada, as portrayed to us by Moorish poets. Indeed, the description of the poet-king Al Motamid, would very well apply to the summer palace of the Governor-General of Algiers.

The same features characterize Moorish architecture everywhere. An airiness and irregularity of construction, a minuteness and floridness of detail, space, loftiness, and light in plenty, and a constant regard to privacy and seclusion.

If the garden is difficult to describe, with its thickets of myrtle and rose, its fountains and basins of pure marble, its groves of palm and pomegranate, its terraces of brilliant flowers and wonderful vistas of greenery, how much more difficult is the palace?

One feels unable to give any idea of those light colonnades, those marble pillars, those gorgeous pavements, those ceilings rich in flowery arabesques, those pleasant courts with rippling fountains and overhanging trees, those doors, and domes, and arches of burnished wood and gold. You wander about feeling that you are in Kubla Khan's pleasure-house, and loth to leave a scene so new and so enchanted.

Just before coming away we went on to the roof of the palace, and never shall I forget the painfulness of that experience. We put our hands to our eyes feeling as if the glare were indeed blinding them, and we were blinded for a few moments. Nothing but a personal experiment can give any idea of what an African sky can be as seen from the roof of an African house; the breadth of white wall and the dazzle of unclouded sunlight on the effect of the perfectly unexperienced eye, beggars description. I think I would almost as soon submit to a surgical operation as ascend the terrace of the Governor-General's palace at Mustapha again. My eyes ache even to think of it.

These pleasant days came to an end early in April, when I was obliged to say adieu to beautiful Algeria and set my face towards Europe.

Chapter 13.

KABYLE VERSUS ARAB.—TRIUMPHS OF FRENCH COLONISTS.—
ARAB INCENDIARIES.—WAHABEE INFLUENCE.—FRUIT-
FULNESS OF THE TELL.—THE PLAGUE OF LOCUSTS.

 PROPOSE in these last chapters to
give as good an idea as I can of the
climate and social condition of Algeria, feeling that such a supplement may be
more welcome to many than any more experiences of my own.

I will begin with saying something about
the European colonists. As is universally
known, the colony of Algeria is not a strong
point with the French residents there. They
feel it to have been a failure hitherto, and
shake their heads when speaking of the future
whether friendly to Arab ascendancy, Kabyle
civilization, or the Imperial notion of turning
Algeria into a vast military training school.

It is the rarest thing to find intelligent Algerians hopeful with regard to their adopted country. " The colonists are not such men as have colonized Australia or New Zealand," they say; " seldom men of pluck, seldomer still men of capital, and they don't come out here with their Lares and Penates, intending to settle themselves and their families. They only come when driven by sheer need, and always with the view of earning a little money and returning to France. *Marseilles is, in fact, too near.*"

" Opposite to Marseilles," said Napoleon the Third in 1852, " we have a vast kingdom to assimilate to France ;" but it was not to be expected that the task would prove an easy one with so many antagonistic elements to subdue. In fact, as on many another occasion, what with his Algerian subjects who were fighting for the Kabyles, and those who were fighting for themselves, the Imperial arbitrator on Algerian affairs must have found himself between two fires, and often hot ones too.

It was impossible to give the Arabs a friendly pat on the shoulder, but a host of philanthropists, political economists and colonists are down upon him, holding up the grievances inflicted upon humanity and themselves by such undue partiality, and showing what a faithless and perverse generation he has chosen to honour.

Of the Arabs I shall have a few words to say by and by, but meantime let us listen to the complaints of the colonists. In the first place, it must be taken for granted your colonist is a hard-worked, much-enduring, one-idea'd man, who has built himself a hut and labours to support a large family on a few acres of land, miles and miles from a market; and not a wealthy owner of orange-gardens, or purchaser of pleasure farms within a ride of Algiers.

This is what the poor colonist will say:

" We have no fault to find with the soil,— that is to say, when the palmetto has been fairly rooted out of it, which is no easy task; but the Arabs burn our crops, and we have no roads to a good market; we are overdone with taxes, and if we try to increase our gains by buying more land, the Arabs we employ won't earn their wages, and the tenants we let it to can't pay rent. There is nothing to do but live from hand to mouth, and wait for better times."

Two or three years back an ardent crusade was preached against the French colonization of Algeria, the reaction of which is felt now. It was urged that the Arab was the labourer *par excellence*, of Algerian soil, that the colonist did not work, that he succumbed to the unsuitability of the climate,—in fine, that in spite of enormous sacrifices made by the government in his behalf, the result was a failure. The Arab was represented as a martyr, and there was much talk about a restricted occupation and a native supremacy. Now it is the Kabyles for whom the cudgels are taken up, and as their cause goes hand in hand with that of the colonists, the majority are content.

It seems to me that the colonists deserve all the good that is said of them, and little of the evil. Such villages as Bonfarik and Ouled el Aleig, on the way to Blidah, could tell stories of heroism passing those of any military campaign. These fertile spots, which for verdure and cultivation would delight the heart of a Suffolk farmer, were mere fever-beds and marshy swamps in the early days of the colony, and heavy and heartsore have been the battles by which they were won to fruitfulness. Three generations of brave pioneers fell victims to the task ; but neither miasma, nor incendiaries, nor Arab raids deterred them from their purpose, and the result glorifies it. Numerous other villages might be named, which the labours of the colonists only have made habitable and healthy, but these two excel others in fertility.

The subject of Arab incendiaries is a sore one with these hard-worked farmers ; and no wonder ! It is hardly to be supposed that a very good understanding should exist between the colonists and natives, especially when we take into consideration of what a mixed set the former consist. French, Germans, Alsatians, Spaniards, Maltese, and occasionally Americans, make up the colonist population ; each and all naturally prejudiced against men who worship Mahomet and marry two wives. But doubtless their antipathy is fully shared by the Arabs, and at any rate, they take a very antagonistic part towards the representatives of the conquered race, stealing their cattle and burning their crops without remorse.

I have before me a copy of the official report of the Commission of Inquiry into the Conflagrations of 1860, 1863, and 1865, of which I will make free use whilst upon this subject. It appears from this report, that the conflagrations have generally taken place at the same time, and have originated from the same motive, namely, hatred of the Christians. The sect of the Wahabees dominating in Arabia, has leavened all Islamism with a new spirit; and in Algeria there are many religious sects who form secret societies, as it were, against the unbelieving, and originate the crusades from time to time. In the records of the assize at Blidah last year, M. le Procureur Impériale made the following statement :

"On the 25th of August fourteen fires appeared simultaneously; on the same day fires raged in the province of the East, where the great forests are to be found. Everywhere is recognised the hand of the incendiary. *They would fain obtain by fire what they have not been able to do by arms.*"

It is more especially in the province of Constantine that this scourge is felt, and a petition was sent to the Emperor in 1865, which states the case for the colonists better than I can do it by a mere abridgment of facts. But as the subject may not interest all my readers, I will put it in the form of a note.*

* *"Constantine, le* 30 *Mai,* 1865.

"SIRE,

"Le domaine forestier de la province de Constantine pour les forêts de chênes-lièves seulement comprend environ 300,000 hectares.

"Cent trente mille déjà concédés à des fermiers, sont aujourd'hui en exploitation. Plus de 10 millions de francs ont été dépensés jusqu'à ce jour dans ces exploitations; la majeure partie est restée entre les mains des indigènes qui sont employés aux travaux.

"Ces 10 millions, qui doivent attendre dix années avant de produire un intérêt quelconque, ont servi à créer, pour l'Etat, un domaine forestier d'une valeur considérable, et pour l'industrie des produits qui forment l'élément le plus actif de la colonisation.

"Cette richesse publique, Sire, la fortune de ceux qui l'ont constituée, est incessamment menacée par la torche des incendiaires.

"En 1860, d'immenses incendies ont dévoré plus de 10,000 de hectares exploités; aucune punition n'a frappé ceux qui les avaient allumés.

"En 1863, d'autres, plus considérables encore ont porté la mine dans les forêts de MM. le Comte de Montebello, Vicomte du Bonchage, Berthon, Duprat, Lucy et Falcon, Chappon, Baron de Marcuil et Dutreile.

That the incendiaries are prompted by malice there can be no doubt. "If we can't fight out the French, we'll burn them out," say the Arabs, and many a poor colonist has literally been burned out. At first sight a

"Le répression se fait encore attendre. Cette impunité, Sire, n'est-elle pas une sorte d'encouragement pour l'avenir? *Ce qui a été épargné jusqu'à présent perira si avant de quitter l'Algérie Votre Majesté n'accorde une protection toute spéciale aux forêts de l'Etat, et ne fait connaître son intention immuable de punir, avec la dernière rigueur, ceux qui y porteraient atteints.*

"Les indigènes, Sire, ne comprennent certainement pas que la ruine des forêts est leur propre ruine. Sans parler des millions qui est passé dans leurs mains, le travail forestier permanent leur assure une rémunération que l'administration forestière évalue à 9f. 30c. par hectare et par an.

"L'industrie des lièges est incontestablement celle de toutes qui crée le plus de rapports entre l'Européen et l'indigène, et prépone le plus sûrement l'assimilation des deux races.

"C'est au nom des intérêts de l'Etat, de ceux de ses fermiers auxquels il doit protection, c'est aussi au nom des intérêts bien entendus des populations indigènes, que nous venons, Sire, pleins de confiance dans la sollicitude dont Votre Majesté donne tant d'épreuves à l'Algérie, appeler son attention sur cette question forestière qui résume de si grands intérêts.

"Nous sommes," &c.

plausible case might be found for the incendiaries, since the custom of burning wooded districts has always been resorted to by Arabs, in order to drive away wild beasts, to clear the earth ready for cultivation, and to renew the pasturage.

But at no epoch, neither under the government of Abd-el-Kader, nor under that of the Turks, nor even in those countries where the native population has been free to act according to its caprice, has fire been resorted to, whether for the renewal of pasture, the expulsion of wild beasts, or the clearing of the soil, whilst the south wind or sirocco was blowing. And why? Because at that time it is impossible to limit or direct the ravages of the fire, so that flocks and men are put in danger.

Clearly then the Arabs are often losers by their own acts of devastation, and it would be hard to find any other motive so likely as that imputed to them.

In this same report of the Commission of Inquiry, is an extremely interesting statement made by an Arab prisoner, before the Council of War of Algiers, in November 1845, which throws some light on the state of feeling entertained by the subordinate for the ruling race.

The individual under examination had been taken prisoner in open revolt, led by his brother; and as he was entirely in the hands of his captors, he was as likely to speak truth as falsehood.

The following questions were put to him:

Query. " Of what did the disaffected tribes reproach the French? — of theft, of exactions, of injustice? Speak the truth without fear."

Prisoner. " Nothing of that kind. The Arabs hate you because you have not the same religion as themselves; because you are strangers; because you have just taken possession of their country, and to-morrow will covet their maidens and children. They said to my brother (the leader of the revolt), 'Lead us, let us begin the war again; each day that passes gives strength to the Christians; let us have done with them at once.'"

Query. " Nevertheless, we have plenty of

Arabs who know how to appreciate us, and are devoted to us."

Prisoner. "There is only one God; my life is in His hands, and not in yours. I will therefore speak freely. Every day you see Mussulmans come to you, who say that they are your faithful servants, and that they love you; don't believe them. They lie either from fear or from interest. Whenever a chief arises whom they believe capable of defeating you, they will all follow him, were it to attack you in Algiers."

Query. "But how? The Arabs have neither army, nor guns, nor money."

Prisoner. "Victory comes from God; when He wills, He makes the weak triumph over the strong."

Query. "Your brother takes the title of Sultan, the Arabs must laugh at it."

Prisoner. "No, they don't laugh at it at all; they love him because of his courage and generosity; for he does not dream, like Abd-el-Kader, of building forts to hold his money and his followers: he understands much better the sort of war to make with you; he but possesses a tent and three good horses. To-day

he is here; to-morrow twenty leagues off;
one moment his tent is full of booty, another
empty. He gives away everything, absolutely
everything, and keeps his hands free that he
may be ready to fly wherever the Mussulmans
call him."

One cannot read a page in Algerian history without coming upon the same sort of
hero, and new ones are constantly rising up
to fan the flame of insurrection and religious
enthusiasm among the followers of the Prophet.

Sometimes these fires are of awful extent; for instance, that of last year on the
frontiers of Tunis, which raged for five days
and nights over an extent of two hundred and
fifty leagues, destroying forests, woods, orchards,
stubble, fodder, and, in many places, dwelling-
houses, and farms with all their stock. But
one is even more touched by such accounts of
private suffering as occasionally reached one's
ears.

I knew a colonist who had purchased a little
land, built himself a house, and was burned, as
the phrase goes, " out of house and home," just
when things were going a little smoothly with

him.   He was a person of considerable education and quite a philosopher; and his way of
reproaching his persecutors reminded me of Sir
Isaac Newton's " Oh, Diamond, Diamond, thou
little knowest the mischief thou hast done !"
When he had built himself another house, and
the Arabs stole his goats and poultry, his remark was, " They wanted them more than I;"
but this easy way of taking things does not
make the case better for the colonists who are
not philosophers.

Anything and everything can be done with
the region of the Tell, that is to say, that
fertile area confined to the plains along the
coast, which was once the granary of Europe.
The Arabs have a proverb, " The Tell is our
mother; whoever be her lord, he is our father;"
and a fruitful mother, indeed, is this lovely
land, abounding, as she does, with corn, and
olives, and fruit.

Traversed by water-courses, and with a
climate tempered by winter rains and fresh
winds blowing from the sea, the Tell is alike a
pleasant place of exile and a fruitful field for
speculation.   Cotton, which, according to Arab
historians, formerly covered the fields of Algeria,

has been cultivated with success; tobacco, flax, hemp, and silk flourish equally, and epicures, who like dainty vegetables all the year round, should come to Algiers, if only to taste the celery and cauliflowers!

Then there are the fruits! How is it possible to describe the figs, the melons, the dates, the olives, the bananas, and, above all, the oranges of Blidah? And the game! The Algerian settler can deck the walls of his hut with skins of hyæna, jackal, gazelle, and panther, the spoils of his gun; can heap his board with steaks of wild boar, with hare, with quails, with snipes, and all kinds of savoury birds; can, in fine, have sport and spoil without end, whether he inhabit the mountainous coast or far-stretching plain. His pastures, covered as they are with flowers, abound in wild honey; his ponds with turtles and tortoises; one might fill a book with a bare list of the good things which are within his reach.

But there are one or two drawbacks I have not yet mentioned. Earthquakes are not uncommon, and now and then occurs such a plague of locusts as we read of in the Bible.

I don't think I can do better than finish this chapter by copying a letter received from Algiers just after I left it last spring:—

"*Mustapha Supérieure, Algiers,*
"*April 26th,* 1866.

"I am sure you will be sorry, dear M——, to hear of the calamity that has befallen our pleasant Algiers, and that the poor people are altogether desolated and despairing, so unexpected has it come upon them.

"In the midst of this lovely weather, when everything was looking so luxuriant and beautiful, the vegetables in perfection, the flowers blooming everywhere, the fields promising an early and abundant harvest,—when all was hope and cheerfulness, THE LOCUSTS HAVE COME!

"I much fear that all this beauty and abundance will be turned into a bare and arid wilderness, and my heart aches for the ruined and starving people we shall soon leave behind. There were rumours last week that the locusts had reached the plain of the Metidja, and had there committed some ravages, but it was hoped that the wind might change and drive them into the sea. Last Thursday morning one of our maids—little Katharine—whom you know, came running into my room, looking white and ghastly, and crying, " Les sauterelles! les sauterelles!" I rushed to the window and saw what looked to be some small glittering birds flying over Madame Bodichon's lower field. It was the beginning of a great storm. They came in millions and trillions of billions! I can give you no idea of their numbers. The air was full of them. It was like a black hailstorm of the largest hailstones you ever saw. If you could only have seen the wondrous sight!

" In a moment, as it were, the whole population were in a state of frightful excitement, and many were weeping aloud. Poor little Katharine's heart was all but breaking for the expected desolation of her father's and brothers' little farms. The people turned out shouting, screaming, beating kettles and frying-pans with sticks and stones, firing guns, and waving handkerchiefs, to prevent the destroyers from settling on their field. This has been going on around Algiers during the last few days till the poor people are quite worn out.

Some have had soldiers to help them, but all in vain. The advanced guard seen in front were speedily increased to an enormous army till nothing else could be seen. Soon they began to settle, and the work of destruction went on apace. They have devoured our neighbour, M. S——'s fine crop of potatoes and peas; but it is much worse for the small farmers like poor Katharine's people, who have lost all their wheat, besides vegetables. I am so sorry for them. The Bouzareah and the fertile slopes of Mustapha, which you know so well, are all bare now. I much fear the poor people will suffer from famine.

"Such a visitation of locusts has not befallen Algiers for twenty-two years; it was a strong wind from the Desert that brought them here. A lady just come from Laghouat tells us that they were lying many inches deep on the road through which they drove.

"Just now the air is so thick with them that it is quite unpleasant to be out. You have to keep waving your parasol to keep them off your face, and they alight on your skirt, and stick there by means of their hooked feet. In look they are like immense grasshoppers, with yellow and green bodies, as long and thick as your middle finger. Dr. B—— tells us that each female lays ninety eggs. The weather is close and warm, with sirocco blowing. We only hope for a strong wind to come and blow them into the sea. The children run about all day catching the locusts and sticking them on long pins; at first, the sight horrified us, but the creatures cause so much suffering that one gets hardened to it. Thousands and hundreds of thousands are caught so, but what is that out of thousands and thousands of millions?

" *April* 29.—The locusts keep coming in great clouds and disappear for awhile. To-day, from early morning till one o'clock, they were thicker than ever, and in those few hours have done a great deal of mischief. We had a thunder-storm last night, but little rain; had it fallen in torrents, it would have been a blessing, for the poor people are in dread now of the sickness that usually follows a swarm of locusts. We leave for Europe in a few days, and are glad of it, for it makes one's heart sick to witness so much misery one is powerless to alleviate!

"Fortunately the plague is one of rare occurrence!

"And now good-bye and *au revoir!* How sorry I am that our golden days in Algeria should have had such a deplorable ending!

"B."

Chapter 14.

IT is impossible to live among the Arabs
for ever so short a time and not grow
deeply interested in them. In Algiers, whether you will or not, you are constantly thrown among these handsome, picturesque, melancholy sons of Ishmael; and though
Mr. Palgrave assures us that the Arab of North
Africa is a very mongrel creature at best,
his idiosyncrasies are marked and worthy of
study.

Take, for instance, my friend Madame

——'s servant Hamet.   He is a handsome, intelligent lad of sixteen, and has lived in her service for several years.   I think it would be hard to find a European youth of the same age whose character could better bear inspection. Devoted to his mistress, though with no stupid canine devotedness, honest, intelligent, and obliging, Hamet wins a good word from every one, and makes himself valuable because he can do his duty without growing conceited about it.   But how far has European influence modified his religious notions?   That is the most interesting point to determine.   From all that I saw of Hamet and other Arabs living in a European domestic atmosphere, I should say that the Mussulman faith waxes weaker in proportion to the cosmopolitan influence exercised upon it.   There is no inclination to proselytism, no expressed lukewarmness of belief, but by little and little the religious practices imposed by the Prophet are disregarded till the once rigid Mahometan becomes a very free-thinker indeed.   The French government very wisely puts its veto upon any kind of interference with the religious practice of the conquered race.   If you enter a mosque, or sacred koubba, without taking off your shoes, you are shown to the door with the most uncompromising rigidity. If you drop in upon a seller of fruits or shoes at his prayers, he goes on till the end without heeding your intrusion. On the Mahometan Sabbath you are positively shut out of the mosques altogether; and during the striking ceremonies of the Ramadhan, but set a step upon the sacred carpet on which the followers of the Prophet are kneeling and you are immediately and sternly reproved!

To show how systematically this French spirit of toleration is carried out, I will repeat an incident that happened to myself. I was travelling by rail to Blidah, in company with a German lady and her Swiss husband, when a very intelligent and talkative Jesuit priest came into our compartment. My friend was a Lutheran, her husband a Roman Catholic, and naturally enough the conversation turned upon religion.

Our fellow-traveller was the director of a seminary near Blidah, which appeared to be in a very prosperous state. He seemed to think the prospects of his Church very prosperous too, even smacking his lips when discussing the Claydon commotions, as if the subject had a sweet savour.

"And the Arabs?" asked the Swiss, "are they to be converted to the true faith?"

The Jesuit shook his head somewhat sadly.

"We are not allowed to try, monsieur, voilà!"

"But do you think trying would be of any good?"

Another shake of the head.

"The Kabyles I have hopes of, but the Arabs are true children of perversion, and will never make good Christians. That is my opinion."

"I notice here," continued the other, "that all Catholic priests grow their beards. Why is this?"

"Ah," answered the Father, with a smile, "you would never guess. Think of it, monsieur, we are obliged to grow beards because the Arabs would have no respect for beardless priests, and would call us a set of old women!"

Of course it is very difficult to get at the real state of religious opinions among the natives, without a thorough knowledge of their language and a long residence among them.

Still it is quite possible to arrive at some clear idea of the different phases and developments of Mahometanism in Algeria by means of books and the experience of others. Whilst there is no doubt that foreign culture has inoculated a part of the community of Algiers with a spirit of laxity and unbelief, the fact is equally patent to all that the puritanic sect of the Wahabees extends its influence to isolated tribes and communities in every part of the conquered province.

Mecca is, in fact, to this day, a hot-bed of conspiracy against Christian influence; and it is generally believed that to fanatic pilgrims and fraternities are due those outbreaks and plots which from time to time disturb the peace of Algerian society.

Every good Mahometan ought to make the pilgrimage to Mecca once in his life. The French government helps him to the fulfilment of this religious duty by running boats from Algiers to Alexandria. A French writer, M. Duvernois, writes rather warmly on the subject of such complacency.

Let the Arabs go to Mecca if they like, he says, but let them do it at their own expense and risk; we surely need not encourage them. We must be very *naïve* to imagine that they sound our praises over the tomb of the Prophet, which is, in truth, the very furnace of fanaticism. Those Frenchmen, they say, only look at them; they think our religion so sublime that they do it homage by helping us on our way here!

Will the Koran give way to the Bible? One cannot say. Foreign influence will doubtless modify many of its institutions, but it seems that the fundamental tenet, " There is but one God, and Mahomet is his Prophet," is likely to last as long as the language in which it was first uttered.*

It is quite certain that the influence of the priests and marabouts is as strong as ever, and that the greater part of Arabs you meet with are orthodox in keeping three out of the five

* " Der objektive semitische Geist, so lang er seine Originalität bewahrt, scheint sich an Mysterien nicht bequemen zu wollen. Die Lehre von einer Dreieinigkeit und einem gekreutzten Gottes Sohn macht daher auf die Araber nie einen bleibenden Eindruck, und wenn sie Eingang fand, war sie immer sehr oberflächlich aufgefasst worden."

See Dr. Sprenger, " Das Leben und die Lehre des Mohammed." Erster Band, p. 16, et seq.

commandments of their sacred book, namely, prayer, almsgiving, and fasting. The other two are pilgrimage and the declaration of faith.

Nothing can be done by a spirit of proselytism. Many and many an intelligent Arab have I heard nip a religious discussion in the bud by saying, " To each his own religion." Madame Luce, the energetic lady I have before mentioned, who was the first person to think of educating Moorish girls, has succeeded, simply and solely, because she consented at the onset to leave proselytism alone. The religious exercises of her little scholars are attended to, and you are reminded of their orthodoxy by the constant occurrence of a little hand, either cut in paper lying on their embroidery frame, or worn in the form of an amulet round the neck. This symbol of a hand is supposed to have reference to the five principal duties before mentioned, the fore-finger signifying prayer, the second almsgiving, and so on.

Another interesting point to consider, is the combined influence of Islamism and Christianity upon the negroes of Algeria. Experience proves that the Negro makes a very bad

Christian, but an excellent Mahometan; and
I am inclined to think with an original writer
on Algeria before quoted, "that the Soudan
and the whole Negro race will be easier civil-
ized by the Koran than the Bible."

There is a considerable body of Negroes
throughout the country who were brought
thither as slaves, before the general emancipation of 1848.   These harmless creatures live
on the friendliest terms with their former masters, a great number have never quitted them;
and, curious enough, those who prefer independ-
ence to domestic service, invariably choose the
trades that best set off their black skins, such as
whitewashing, baking, bricklaying, selling flour.

And now let us consider the moral qualities of
the Arabs.   Are they really liars, voluptuaries,
dissimulators, sluggards, as represented?   Are
the heroic qualities of bravery, daring, hospitality, and good faith, groundlessly imputed to
them?   Will the glories of Granada revive, and
the glowing epics of Moorish story repeat
themselves?   It is hard to choose between the
conflicting opinions of those more competent
to judge.   Whilst one says, "Hope nothing
from the Arab; he is of a fast fading race like

the American Indian;" another says, "But
persuade the Arab to give up the Koran, and
he may become a useful member of society."
A third will tell you that, Koran or no Koran,
intercourse with Europeans is gradually doing
its work, and that, by-and-by, the Arab will be
a Frenchman.

The great bugbear with all these writers
and talkers is polygamy. A man may beat
his wife, may leave his wife for another woman,
may spend all his substance in drink, and we,
vous autres Chrétiens, as the Arabs call us,
can forgive him, but we can never forgive
the Mussulman his sin of polygamy. With
regard to the Arabs of the Tell, I am inclined
to believe that polygamy is daily becoming
rarer, whilst to the inhabitants of the Sahara,
quite a different rule of criticism must be
applied.

The Arab of the Desert is no luxurious
lord of harems and odalisques. He is to this
day a mighty hunter; an Ishmael agains·
whom everyone's hand is turned; a dweller
in tents. He is always occupied in hunting;
in making a raid against an enemy; in cele-
brating some fantasia of triumph; or in fol-

lowing his chief to battle. The women grind
corn ; tend the young camels and horses ;
prepare the *kous-kous;* weave the burnouses;
dress the camels' skin that forms the curtain
of the tent. All the industrial occupations
fall thus of necessity upon the wife. A man
who should only possess one were in very
poor case indeed. Badly clothed, badly fed,
unable to entertain guests, his tent empty and
ragged, such an individual would be the very
Pariah of his tribe. The woman plays no subordinate part in this primitive and warlike
society.

The men sing as they rush on their enemies. " To-day we will die for the women
of our tribe ;" and when ignoble terms of peace
are proposed, they say, " What will our wives
say if we have not fought ?"

" It is a great mistake," says General
Daumas, " to believe that Islamism keeps women in a state of subjection from which only
miracles of the Christian religion can extri-
cate her. The Mahometan woman, on the
contrary, has preserved among the men her
name urges into the combat such prestige

as was possessed by the Queens of Beauty in
the tournaments of the middle ages."

Love-songs as full of imagery as the Song
of Solomon, and as delicate in sentiment as
the poems of the Arab poets of Spain, abound
to this day, and a handful of these flowers
of the Desert were well worth the plucking.
Whether, as in the golden age of Moorish
supremacy in Spain, you find for every Ca-
tullus a Sappho, I know not.   But we read
how in those days, a woman of genius and
cultivation was not seldom more courted than
the most renowned beauty ; and poet and
poetess sometimes sent love-letters to each
other in verse which was worthy to come down
to us.

But one is a long way removed from the
poetry of the Sahara at Algiers, though here
one finds poetic suggestion enough.

Never shall I forget how, on the occasion
of General Jussuf's funeral, a crowd of fine-
looking chiefs flocked into the city.   They
wore scarlet burnouses, white linen turbans
bound by camel's hair, mocassins of crimson
leather, and only wanted arms and yataghans
to make a splendid picture.   As it was, they

sat very peacefully outside the *cafés*, drinking coffee, their superb figures looking as unlike the pale dwarfed Europeans around them, as if they were of a wholly different genus. Certainly for physical beauty and nobility of movement, the Arab stands alone of all the races in the world.

The women are for the most part wanting in equal grace of feature and form, but how can one wonder at it, seeing the sedentary and secluded life they lead? It used to rejoice my heart to see the omnibuses and streets full of them on Fridays, when they went to the cemeteries to hold intercourse with the dead, and thus gained a little fresh air.

New-comers to Algiers soon catch a prevalent habit of speaking contemptuously of the Arabs, especially with regard to their intellectual qualities.

The Kabyle is the good boy, the Arab the bad boy, of the large and heterogeneous family adopted by the French; and it was only because the Emperor inclined favourably towards the latter, that such a shoal of pamphlets and books of an anti-Arab tendency appeared after his visit. Very likely a reaction

will occur before long, but in the meantime
it is worth while to inquire whether the Arabs
of Algeria are really the effeminate, dissimu-
lating, lying, gaming set they are represented
to be.

From all that I have seen, heard, and
read of them, I should say, No; and I
think that everything is to be hoped from a
freer and fuller intermixture with Europeans.
We may be quite certain that there exist no
surer means of counteracting Wahabee bigotry
than that of unconditional and friendly intercourse between the French and Arab inhabitants of Algeria.

It is astonishing to find how many super-
stitions regarding the Arabs linger in the
minds of highly cultivated people.   For instance, no sooner does an artist set foot in
Algiers than he is told, "Oh! of what good
is it for an artist to come here? The Mahometans think drawing a sin, and you'll get
no sitters,"—and sitters are indeed difficult
to get; but the difficulty often arises from a
very different cause to that expressed.

It is easy to understand how a people so
wedded to domestic privacy, so jealous of their

women, so averse to innovations, should set themselves against foreign artists and thwart their wishes in every possible way. A reputable Moorish woman will not unveil to her brother-in-law; an Arab, or Moor of the very lowest class, would not allow his wife or grown-up daughter to sit as a model, but, in both cases, the prejudice is not so much religious as social. Among those better educated Mahometans, who have mixed with Europeans, one finds the photographic *carte de visite* almost as common as in England, and it is daily becoming more common.

The prettiest and most luxurious Moorish house I ever visited in Algiers, that of the director of the `Collége Arabe, was adorned with pictures of Mecca, plans of Medina, and other religious subjects. Some of the native merchants present their customers, as a parting souvenir, with their *carte de visite;* and one of the most admired portraits in my album is that of a handsome, intelligent, and genial Arab, of whom I bought a few knicknacks, which he himself gave me at parting.

The sum-total of Mahomet's veto upon art is contained in the fifth book of the Koran.

"Oh, believers," he says, " wine, gambling, statues, and casting of lots, are abominations invented by Satan. Abstain from them and you shall be happy ;" and though the same sentiment was expressed in his Conversations, there is no ground for the sweeping assertion that the founder of Islam excluded every art from his followers but architecture. What do facts teach us? Has no Mahometan Rubens or Tintoretto arisen for the glory of Islam? Could a race produce such architecture, such poetry, such philosophy, and no Canova?

If we are not able to answer these questions satisfactorily, and claim for Muslim artists a high place, we are at least able to prove their existence. Out of numerous instances, let us take two or three.

The Fatimides possessed portraits of all their celebrated men, and decked their tents with statues, whilst in their treasuries were elegant porcelain dishes on which were represented armed men, figures of animals, etcetera.

In the middle of the eleventh century, a vizier lived at the court of the Caliph, at Cairo, who especially loved and encouraged the arts. Amongst the painters whom he gathered about him were two rivals of great renown, named Kassir and Ibn Aziz, who were clothed in robes of honour, and rewarded with purses of gold.

In the same city was a picture of another artist, Al Kitami, representing Joseph at the well, greatly celebrated for its life-like expression and colour. Makrizi, the Arabic historian of the fourteenth century, quotes a work in his own language, "On the Different Schools of Painting;" and Ibn Bahuta, another Muslim author, tells of an African king who went to the mosque daily under a canopy decorated with birds fashioned in pure gold.

Arabic manuscripts are to be found beautifully illuminated, and adorned with pictures representing incidents of life and adventure, whilst the Escurial possesses an exquisite work of Ibn Zafer, a Sicilian Arab, which is profusely illustrated.

Many copies of the narrative of Abou'l Kasem Hasiri are adorned with appropriate pictures, such as a slave-market, the halt of a caravan in the desert, an assembly of tolfers, and other subjects of daily life.

Granted, then, that the artistic faculty was by no means wanting among the Arabs, what has hindered them from attaining such excellence in painting and sculpture as they have done in literature and philosophy? The arguments of a German writer, Adolf von Schach, which are entirely in favour of a subjective hindrance, and do not seek it beyond the idiosyncrasy of the Arab intellect seem the most plausible. We find that in spite of the Prophet's denunciation of wine, the court poets of the Caliph made it their chief theme, and it was the same with music, the dance, and singing. Within a century after the Hegira, the Palaces of the Commander of the Faithful resounded with musical instruments, songs, and dancing, and to the present day the Moorish dancing-girl attracts crowds wherever she goes.

The cause, therefore, must be sought elsewhere than in the pages of the Koran; and I think may be found in a deficiency of the otherwise so richly endowed Arab intellect, which has hindered it from bringing the creative form of poetry to higher perfection.

" The Arab," says Schach, "does not represent to himself all the pictures of the outer world in sharp and distinct outlines; he gazes at them through a shifting mist of clouds. . . . When he represents the phases of nature and human life, he invariably gives rather the impression than the image of what he has seen. . . . he also wants that gift which enables one to see a single object with all its parts and in all its relations as a whole. In all these points the Arab and Semitic races generally stood in sharp contrast to the Greeks; for, whilst to the latter the plastic faculty was granted in the highest degrees, so that they clothed every dream in tangible shape, as the clearness, the unity, the strength of form and subordination of all parts to one whole, of all their dramatic and creative art, testify, the Arabs drew the outer world subjectively, had little understanding for form and outline, for uniformity and general perception, and could, therefore, never get beyond the elements of sculpture and painting, or epic and dramatic poetry."

But I must leave this interesting subject, which I hope to take up some other day. May the Fates grant me another sojourn in Al-gezira, the White City, that I may there

renew my Arab lessons, sitting in a Moorish
garden, and writing, with a reed pen, the
Psalms of the Koran, or the adventures of the
far-travelled Ibn-Bahuta!

With regard to the present condition of the
Arabs of Algeria, there can hardly be a doubt.
The Arab of the interior may hate the Frank
or Roumi, but he hated the Turk worse, and
the industrious Moor, who reaps a harvest
during the influx of winter visitors, has hardly
grounds for hating the Christians at all.

There is a marked distinction between the
physiognomy of the Moor and Arab. The
Moor is a little above middle height and inclined to stoutness, his face is oval and slightly
effeminate, with olive complexion, large brilliant eyes, aquiline nose, and full lips. The
Arab is tall and well knit, with straight nose,
receding forehead, lively black eyes, finely-
shaped mouth, splendid complexion, abundant
beard, and a melancholy expression. The
Moor is the fine gentleman of Algiers, *par excellence.* He is always dainty in his dress, and
scrupulously clean, and has the character of
being very religious, and rather indolent. The
Arab marching along in his white burnous

makes a far more imposing figure, but is not nearly so sociably disposed towards strangers; though there is little doubt that in nine cases out of ten, he has every reason to thank the conquest.

The thing speaks for itself, since the price of all the products of the country has reached the sextuple of former years. Before the conquest, the cereals of the Metidja were of so little value, that unsold sacks of corn were left in the market-place till the following week, —and this in a country of thieves!

Again, the poor Arab who formerly let himself by the year, gaining the crumbs from his master's table, and a burnous, worth from fifteen to thirty francs, as payment in kind for the twelve months, now earns from the colonists a franc and a half to two and a half per day, according to his skill or the season.

A third fact speaks still more plainly. Under the Turkish rule the *serrual* or Moorish *culotte* in the interior distinguished the higher ranks of the military only. When a hero was celebrated in verse, it was said, " The *monalin es-serrual*, the wearers of *culottes*, have done such and such prodigies of bravery." Now-a-days every one is well enough off to wear this article of dress.

The Arab is a very poor farmer and a worse economist. He sells his corn or his wool just when they are ready, not waiting, as we do in Suffolk, "till markets are up," and then buries his money in a hole.

It has been calculated by a writer on Algerian affairs that were this buried capital collected and put out to interest, the Arabs would divide an interest of forty millions of francs. Instead of this, the seller of corn, sheep, wool, and oxen, to the amount of ten thousand francs, looks out for a corner and buries his money in the dead of the night, hoping to leave it undisturbed till another year.

Before the conquest,—can it be believed?—it was the custom to lay up corn against bad years in pits. Every one remembers Pharaoh's dream, which Joseph explained to him, but it may be novel to learn that, up to the present day, it has been the custom in North Africa to follow Joseph's example and lay up corn for times of drought.

" The seven good kine are seven years, and

the seven good ears are seven years; the dream is one.

"And the seven thin and ill-favoured kine that came up after them, are seven years; and the seven empty ears blasted with the east wind shall be seven years of famine."

Thus spoke the Patriarch, and owing to the unscientific farming of the Arabs, and their incapability of modifying climatical influences, many a seven years' plenty has been followed by a seven years' famine since.

When the French first came to Algiers all the tribes had stores of wheat laid up sufficient for ten years ; but there is no doubt that the example of the colonists in draining, manuring, and changing the courses of the crops will in time be generally followed.

The constitution of Arab society offers many complications at first sight, especially when viewed in relation to the government. One gets confused as to the weight of dignity expressed by the word Kaïd, Agha, Bach-Agha, Kadi, Cherif, Marabout, Tholba, Cheik, etcetera.

Without going into unnecessary and wearisome descriptions, it is incumbent upon any writer on Algeria to explain the most important of these titles.

The Kaïd is chosen from the tribe, and exercises considerable power, much restricted, of course, since the establishment of *bureaux Arabes.* He is charged with the interior police, and is responsible for the execution of all law, whether administered by the French bureaux, or the chief of the tribe, or cheik.

The Bach-aghas and Aghas are named by the Minister of War, and exercise military power solely. The Kadi is entrusted with civil power, draws up marriage settlements, grants divorce, and administers estates. Many and many a time have I seen the Kadi judging in the little court behind the great mosque at Algiers. He was an elderly, indolent, aristocratic-looking man with a beautiful white beard, and performed his office very leisurely, lying upon a divan, amid a crowd of turbaned lawyers and pleaders.

Once a woman was petitioning for divorce. We could not see her during the trial, but her voice came shrill and loud from an aperture in the wall, and when all was over, she waddled away with her negress mumbling and mouthing discontentedly enough.

Then a negro came up, the blackest negro I have ever seen in my life, and said his say. He wore white drawers, a pink gandoura or shirt, and yellow flowers behind his ears; and as he stood in the bright sunlight thus decorated, his unmitigated luminous blackness was quite beautiful. One was reminded of the story in the "Thousand and One Nights," and fancied that like the first calendar, the Prince of the Four Black Isles, this negro had been turned into ebony by enchantment. It seemed impossible to regard such jetty polish and solidity as mere everyday flesh and blood.

Perhaps the most important title and rank of all, is that of the *Marabout*, or member of the religious aristocracy. This class is well worthy of study from all points of view.

The marabout, or priest, more than any one, keeps back the tide of foreign innovation; it is he who preaches war against the heretics; he who preserves intact the most pernicious traditions of the Mahometan faith, and as his influence is as strong as ever, and he seems more than ever inclined to preserve it, one may well hesitate before hoping too much for the Arab.

The lists and legends of marabouts are endless, and, in every town and village, you meet with a tomb consecrated to the memory of some miracle-working saint. These shrines, or *marabouts*, as they are confusedly called, are hung with costly reliquiæ of the departed, and are open from morning till night.

Nothing can equal the deference paid by the Arabs to these quasi-priests. I remember once seeing a very venerable old man lounging about with a lovely little child of about seven years. One always longs to play with pretty children, and I gave this little girl an orange by way of beginning an acquaintance. When about to question her old protector as to her name and age, a very poor-looking Arab plucked my sleeve and whispered, "Marabout." So I felt reproved and was silent.

Education is, of course, the only means of counteracting this pernicious priestly influence. Only let a few more ladies follow in the steps of Madame Luce, and Moors and Arabs be generally tempted into having their boys taught with the sons of Europeans, and the marabout orthodoxy would gradually disappear.

The marabout must not be confounded with the imam, who is the officiating priest at prayer-time, at funerals, and at sacred festivals; his influence is, however, very subordinate.

The above-mentioned institution of *bureaux Arabes* offers complexities that have been amusingly described by French authors. These *bureaux Arabes* were organised with a view to protect the native interests; and keep a *surveillance* over the tribes as well. They ought to offer a guarantee that no violence shall be done to the property, faith, and customs of the Mussulmans, and, at the same time, defend the interests of the colonists; but as the task is rather Herculean, one can hardly speak of it as more than attempted.

The commandant of a division perhaps places the administration of these *bureaux Arabes* in the hands of officers, intelligent and well-meaning enough, no doubt, but naturally quite unqualified for the office, and ignorant of the Arabic language.

An interpreter is attached to every *bureau*, but how can one interpreter do the brain-work of several? No wonder that these same *bureaux Arabes* offer material for discontent on all sides, and food for all smart writers on the affairs of the colony.

There is a most amusing book by a former director of a *bureau*,—M. Richard—which gives some idea of the complications, sometimes comic, sometimes grave, that ensue at these little centres of administration. What could be better than the following little scene? An Arab and his wife enter the seat of justice and ask for a divorce. Before the unfortunate *chef du bureau* has time to ask a single question, he is deluged with the following burst of eloquence from both plaintiffs at the same time.

It must be observed that two or three Arabs, when quarrelling or contracting a bargain, all talk at once, so that the burlesque has its rhyme and reason.

Chef du Bureau.	*First Plaintiff.*	*Second Plaintiff.*
	For a man respected as I am to put up with such a state of things! Am I to live with a termagant and a loose woman who scandalizes me to my neighbours? If she only left me a moment's peace in my tent I would wink at many things in consideration of her family! But she makes my home a very pandemonium! I never return but to find her fighting my other wives or my people! Only think! the other day, just because I made the simple remark that my dinner was badly cooked, the saucepan, broth, and even the hot cin-	For a woman looked up to by all the world as I am, to live with such a wretch and become the butt of his brutality, indeed! A ruffian who compromises my good name! If he only led me a quiet life in my tent, by Allah! I'm so good-natured, that I would look over his bad behaviour because of my relationship; for I may as well confess it,— this horrid man is my cousin. Just think! the other day, under the pretence that his dinner was badly cooked, he threw at my head the saucepan, the broth, and even the cinders from the fire. If
How can I understand one word you say? You screech out in a manner to break the strongest tympanums!		
Only listen; for Heaven's sake!		
Be quiet, my good souls, if only to take breath.		
In God's name, hold your tongues. Don't you know that you are not in your own tent?		
Silence, I say, or I shall be com-		

Chef du Bureau.	First Plaintiff.	Second Plaintiff.
pelled to send you away to calm yourselves a little. Upon my word, this is intolerable! Cheik! Insist upon silence. It is impossible to put up with this Babel any longer!	ders of the fire, came at my head! If it hadn't been for a negro who came to my relief, I was a dead man!	a negress hadn't come to my help, I was as good as a dead woman. My body is black and blue from his ill-treatment, and if I were not a modest woman, I'd show you my poor shoulders, which are in such a state as no one would imagine!

Cheik, in a voice of which no human sound can give the faintest idea,—

" Silence!"

There are an infinity of scenes equally curious, and I daresay equally based on personal experience ; and any unfortunate Frenchman placed at the head of one of these *bureaux Arabes* had need be wiser than Solomon and more patient than Job.

The Arabs have a knack of lying one against the other on emergencies, and often a poor little ass will be contended for with such oaths and protestations on either side that it is almost impossible to decide who has sworn and lied most.

Whoever has given any attention to the Arabic language will easily understand that the thousand and one forms of oaths and ejaculations found in it have none of the profanity and vulgarity one is apt to couple with that form of speech. The idiosyncrasy belongs to the language; and however pious or well-bred an Arab may be, he seldom speaks a sentence without an oath.

The every-day life of the Arab, whether he be a Tellian or Saharian, in other words, an inhabitant of the mountainous zone of Algeria in part colonised by Europeans, or a wanderer in the sandy plains of the Sahara, is no longer a mystery to us. You can get quite a little library of French books on this subject in Algiers. But the every-day life of the women is almost as hidden as ever. Yet, as has been already proved, it is quite possible for any European lady of tact to mix with Moorish and Arab women, and if she speak their language, to attain to something like intimacy. There is no computing the revolution that might be effected in the inane life of rich

Moorish ladies or their hard-worked sisters by
such a crusade.

Mahomet does not dwell upon the enjoy-
ments of women in Paradise, but he does not
exclude them from it, as is often supposed ;
and in his so-called *Hadites*, or Conversations,
there are counsels to the beautiful Ayesha, as
to the best means of ensuring eternal happi-
ness.

"If you desire to rejoin me in Paradise,"
he said to her, "supply yourself with the provisions of the humble traveller only, and never
associate with the rich."

In the Koran the beatification of good
women is mentioned more than once, and in the
4th Book he distinctly holds out the hope of
Paradise to the weaker sex.

"Pardon those, O Lord," he says, "who
return to thee and follow thy path.   Save
them from the punishment of flames.   Conduct
them, Lord, into the Garden of Eden, which
thou hast promised them, also to their parents,
their wives, and their children."

Kadijah, the first and best beloved wife of
the Prophet, does not stand alone among Arab
women for decision of character and sound

practical sense. It is true that she persuaded her father to get tipsy because he disapproved of the marriage with her young servant, and during the fit of intoxication married him ; but she was only driven to this *ruse* by the excess of parental authority.

Kadijah has never yet found her biographer, but richly deserves one. Her faith in Mahomet, her eager belief in his inspired character, her unswerving love and encouragement, as related by old Arab chronicles, are touching enough, and there is no doubt that her influence over the Prophet was incalculable. Without such influence, it is to be doubted whether Mahomet would ever have shone before the world as a prophet, and by her death Islam lost much of its purity, and the Koran much of its elevation.*

These old chronicles have a Biblical pathos and simplicity about them, strangely contrasted with the gorgeous and glowing Arab narratives of later times. Take for instance the following :—

The Prophet said, " O Kadijah, when I

* See Dr. Sprenger's work before quoted.

heard the voice and saw the light (speaking of his first visions), I feared that an evil spirit was in me."

Kadijah answered him, " God will not lead thee astray, O son of Abd-Allah!" Then she went to her father Waraka and related the matter to him.

He said, " Thou art right, he is not possessed by an evil spirit. This is an ordinance like the ordinance of Moses. If he maintains his calling whilst I am yet in life, I will stand by him and believe in him."

Another story relating to the same period of the Prophet's life is equally interesting.

When the Prophet was in this condition and found himself in Aggad, he saw an angel sitting on the borders of heaven, who cried, " O Mahomet, O Mahomet, I am Gabriel!" The Prophet was frightened, and as many times as he looked up he beheld the angel again.

He hastened to Kadijah and related the event, and said, " Nothing is so hateful to me as these same false gods and soothsayers. I fear that in the end I shall be a soothsayer."

She said to him, " Ah, say not so, O son of my uncle! God will not forsake thee; thou holdest even part and lot with thy family, thou speakest the truth, thou observest fair dealing and hast a noble character."

When his mind became tranquil, and he believed in his inspired calling, all the traditions make mention of her great contentment and joy.

Coming down to the golden age of Moorish supremacy in Spain, we find that many and many a Corinna and Olympia Morata of pure Arab blood flourished there. Is there any reason for supposing Mahometan women to be entirely without mind and morals now?

Abassa, the sister of the great Al Raschid, had a fine poetical genius. Labana, a Moorish lady of Spain, was not only a poetess, but a philosopher and fine arithmetician; there was an Ayesha, who is honoured by Mussulmans with the title of doctor, for her mental attainments; a royal Ayesha who distinguished herself as a poetess and orator in the twelfth century, and left behind her a splendid library, and many other famous women whom I cannot stay to enumerate.

It is the want of education that keeps these poor creatures in a state of childish incapability, and all honour to those who have made an effort in this cause! It is satisfactory to know that their efforts have been successful on the whole, and that such Moorish children as have been entrusted to them, have showed aptitude in study. Of course the attempt to establish French schools for Moorish children was one of superhuman difficulty, and though at present the instruction is chiefly confined to needlework and embroidery, a step has been made in the right direction.

As is the case all the world over, the weakest go to the wall, and the boys get the education denied to the girls. Whilst the daughters of good Moorish and Arab families are considered sufficiently educated if they can make preserves, and dye their eyes and fingers with henna, the sons go to an excellent college, where they receive the advantages of enlightened and liberal instruction.

This *Collége Français-Arabe* is undoubtedly one of the most hopeful signs for the colony. The lads, taken promiscuously from Moorish, Arab, or Kabyle tribes, cannot fail, associated as they are with intelligent French professors, to become half French too. Destined to fill, perhaps, the posts of caid, agha, ben-hagha, and imam, the importance of their future influence cannot be overlooked,—an influence modified by French intercourse, culture, and mode of life.

Some of these boys are the sons of fierce Bedouin chiefs who lately fought the French so obstinately for years; some were born in the poorest villages of Kabylia; others are Kou-loughlis, or the children of Turkish and Moorish parents.

Many a time have I watched a troop of these little students at play in the Marengo gardens outside Algiers, and a prettier sight could hardly be. They were of all types, the slender oval-faced Arab, the rosy square-built Kabyle, the olive-complexioned Kouloughli, the handsome effeminate Moor, all wearing the same picturesque Zouave uniform of blue *serrual* or *culotte*, crimson sash, vest of brilliant carmine embroidered with gold, and little red Fez caps with long silk tassels. As they played about among the palm-trees, one could not help coveting the privileges they enjoyed for their sisters, and prophesying all sorts of revolutions from such a beginning. There is no doubt that, when these boys grow to manhood, they will find the wives provided for them very insipid and uncompanionable. How, indeed, can it be otherwise?

On the whole, the Arab population of Algeria is more interesting than any other. However slight may be the intercourse one is enabled to hold with them, their attractive qualities of hospitality, politeness, charity, and resignation under misfortune, are sure to come out. One shuts one's ears to the stories of treachery, theft, untruthfulness, and vagabondage, and willingly gives credence to the seductions of legends and traditions. Their history, their religion, their language, and their literature, have too much splendour about them to be forgotten—even when listening to the complaints of the French colonist!

Chapter 15.

S a winter residence for invalids, Algiers offers so many attractions and advantages that this little book must of necessity be imperfect without an especial chapter devoted to them.

Few people realize what a superb climate and lovely country lie within four or five days of London. It is true that the sea has to be crossed twice, but the *Messageries* steamers are so good and the Mediterranean so pleasant in tolerable weather, that no one would regard the two days' voyage from Marseilles to Algiers as an insuperable obstacle. Moreover, sea-sickness is proved curable beyond a doubt, by ice-bags; and this fact may well embolden martyrs to brisk winds and rolling seas, to make an effort in search of a climate.

And how they are rewarded ! To be placed beyond reach of fogs and east winds, to be sure of feeling the sun at least once a-day, to rejoice in a bright blue sky, and drink in a warm spring air from November to April—surely this is worth some sacrifice to the invalid or sickly !

The climate of Algiers as nearly approaches perfection, I should say, as any in the world ; and I have never seen people who came out with hollow cheeks and hard coughs, gaining flesh and vitality every day, without coveting what they enjoyed for all victims to our fogs and March winds.

During the winter of 1865-6, there was not a day when I could not go out, and though residents in Algiers told me that the season was an exceptionally dry one, I believe that the heaviest rains of November and February seldom last more than a few days and then with intermissions, during which one can take exercise. At such times, even in the town, a little fire is acceptable, but no sooner do the clouds disperse, than the windows are thrown open, the pleasant warmth of the sun is felt through the whole frame, and warm clothing becomes unbearable.

Sometimes so early as March or April, the streets of Algiers are hot during the middle of the day; but only take an omnibus or fiacre to St. Eugène, le Frais Vallon, or Mustapha, and you find yourself in the superb atmosphere of an old-fashioned English May or June. The hedges are alive with the songs of starlings and swallows; children are playing under the shade of carob and olive-trees; white-bearded Arabs are selling oranges and basking in the sun; and the sea has hardly a ripple.

Algiers is an eminently cheerful place. There is a pretty little theatre under excellent management, an out-door concert every afternoon in the fine square of the Place du Gouvernement, a reading-room for men, shopping for ladies, a variety of walks in the lovely public gardens, rides on the hills, and agreeable society for all who come out provided with proper introductions.

The hospitality of the Governor-General and Madame la Maréchale de Macmahon, is very liberally extended to English visitors, and there are few people who do not come away with very lively remembrances of the pleasant evenings spent in their pretty Moorish palace.

These assemblies have quite a character of their own on account of the variety of costume. There you see the rich Jewish ladies in their ancestral brocades and silk lace; the stately Caïd or Agha wearing the linen head-dress of the primitive Arab, the white burnous and the crimson mocassins; the turbaned Jew, the handsome, elegant Moor, and an infinity of French uniforms and decorations.

Of course it is difficult to characterise the French society, seeing it, as tourists can only do, from the surface. But a very short experience of French-Algerian society has convinced me that it is leavened by a spirit of intelligence, cultivation, and liberality. I think in very few provincial towns you would find it so easy to get cultivated, sensible, and agreeable people together as in Algiers. Indeed, I have sometimes found such good conversation, such admirable music, such cosmopolitan and refined tastes and interests in small private parties, as to fancy myself in the salons of Vienna, Paris, or London.

It would be impertinent for me to name those whose personal influence has had most effect in organising the society of Algiers, or I would gladly and heartily pay the tribute of acknowledgment to whom it is due. It is sufficient to say that, putting out of question all official hospitality, whether French or English, there are one or two leading spirits in Algiers who largely exercise to both poor and rich the graces of hospitality and such good gifts of kindness as the American poet says, " most leave undone or despise."

A few years ago, a strong socialistic spirit exercised its influence among some French residents, and a Phalanstery was established, which flourished for a little while. There still remain a few believers in Fourier and Enfantin, from whose pens occasionally issue earnest little pamphlets on the doctrine of *Solidarité* or the *Destinée Sociale* of the human race; though I believe the white heat of enthusiasm to be passed.

The Frenchwomen of Algiers deserve a

special chapter. I have already mentioned
Madame Luce, who mastered Arabic, and cou-
rageously set herself to the task of ameliorat-
ing the condition of Moorish women.

Another lady was the main founder of a
society for the prevention of cruelty to animals
—a most necessary institution among a people
so regardless of their beasts as the lower class
of Arabs.

A third, a most interesting and intelligent
young lady, is following in the steps of Dr.
Elizabeth Blackwell and Miss Garrett, and,
if successful, may be a great friend to
Mahometan women; since a little notion of
hygiene would do more towards improving
their condition than all the education in the
world.

Whether regarded from a social, natural,
or climacterial point of view, Algiers, I think,
holds out enticements to all. Idlers can find
distractions as novel as they are varied; artists
can find a field almost new, and full of interest;
students have rich materials at hand, whether
they care to dive into the mysteries of the half-
forgotten language and literature of the Kabyles, or study the Koran and its worshippers;

for the sportsman, there is game in abundance ; for the traveller, adventure ; lastly, for the sickly and the sorrowful, that treasure of all treasures,—health.

Let us consider the climate of Algiers and the natural advantages of its geographical position.

The Greek word κλίμα signifies region or zone of the earth, and thoroughly to understand any climate we must look a little at the astronomical, geographical, and atmospheric influences modifying it.

Any one who carefully studies the map of North Africa will see how highly favoured in every way is this beautiful Algeria, to which we are inviting all those who love the sun.

Lying between 4° 1' west and 6° 2' east longitude, and extending from 34° 1' to 37° 1' north latitude, Algeria partakes of the idiosyncracy of warm and of temperate latitudes ; the days and the nights have a tendency to be equal ; there is no dawn, so to say, and no twilight ; and there are only two seasons, the dry and the rainy.

The features of this κλίμα, or zone, are varied enough, and sufficiently account for the rare fertility of its soil, the geniality of its climate, and the variety of its flora and fauna.

To begin with the Tell, or, more intelligibly speaking, North Algeria. This region may be described as a vast and splendid amphitheatre of cultivated hills, plateaux, and well-watered valleys, stretching along the Mediterranean, and reaching inward for upwards of a hundred and twenty-five miles.

The second region into which Algeria has been divided, namely, the Sahara or South Algeria, reaches from the Tell to the Desert, and consists of high table-lands; the home of tents, of large flocks, and of primitive Arab life.

It is only, however, with regard to its modifying influences on the climate of the Tell that we are now considering the Sahara. For the sirocco that blows from the Desert may be considered the only drawback to the Algerian climate, though that is chiefly felt during the summer months.

The Little Atlas range, which runs parallel to the Mediterranean, extends throughout the whole length of Algeria; breaking the country into basins and valleys, and hindering or imprisoning torrents on their way to the sea.

Cascades are frequent and beautiful, and the plenty of water-courses renders the landscape everywhere verdant and spring-like. There are also numerous salt lakes and hot mineral springs, which latter will doubtless ere long become cheerful little centres of valetudinarianism.

"Look about you," says a doctor learned in the subject of Algerian springs, "in these delicious gorges of the Atlas, and you will find seats of ease that rival Piombières, Spa, Vichy and Seidlitz. Land at Algiers, cross the plains of the Metidja, and you are there."

Sheltered from the fiery atmosphere of the Great Desert, and the radiations of the sea, the climate of the Tell is uniformly mild and genial. Whilst snow lies on the highest peaks of the Atlas during the winter months, it is almost unknown around Algiers, and the abundance of water and sunshine produce unequalled fertility during the most arid months of the year.

There are no east winds, fogs, nor frosts. The air is moist, warm, and light; the sky universally bright and pure. Placed midway between both extremes of temperature, Algeria offers every favourable condition of climate from October to May. Whilst the lover of warm sunshine and soft air will find a second Penzance in the city, there is always a bracing atmosphere on the hills in its immediate neighbourhood, or a little farther off, as at Blidah or Cherchell.*

Wherever he goes he will find a luxuriant and lovely vegetation, through what to us are the dreariest months of the year, namely, December and January. The gardens are full of violets, geraniums, and roses. The hedges are hung with clematis and cyclamen.

People sit out of doors in the evening about the cafés, and throw open their windows to let in the sunlight at first waking. Even in the country, when wood-fires are acceptable at night, the day is always pleasant and warm.

The winter rains generally take place in November and February, and last some days, though there is rarely a day when one cannot

---

* For further information on the climate of Algiers, see the works of Drs. Bodichon, Bertherand, Mitchell, Agnily, Perier, and M. Desprez.

go out. Personally, I cannot speak of this wet season, having had nothing more than occasional April showers during my stay in Algiers from December to April—but then that was considered an exception. On most days one could dress as in June at home. The mean winter temperature of Algiers is 53°. The mean summer temperature is 75°.*

Formerly marsh-fever was the scourge of the Metidja, but owing to effective drainage and planting, some villages have been rendered quite healthy, and there are few where, with proper precautions, the miasma may not be guarded against.

This subject concerns colonists more than tourists, who naturally take up their abode in or near the city, for many reasons.

* I abstract with permission the following table of the mean temperature of Algiers, from a little work published in Algiers some years since :—

		Fahrenheit.		
		8 A.M.	Noon	5 P.M.
1856				
Mean Temperature of first 15 days December		59·43	61·20	60·66
,,	of last 16 ,, ,,	53·40	55·22	54·16
1857	of first 15 days January,	52·86	55·27	54·17
,,	of last 16 ,, ,,	49·25	51·52	42·66
,,	of first 14 days February,	51·64	55·27	54·58
,,	of last 14 ,, ,,	59·04	61·37	60·02
,,	of first 15 days March,	56·30	59·12	51·87
,,	of last 16 ,, ,,	59·66	62·89	60·96

For the benefit of both tourists and colonists, it may be broadly stated, that the climate of Algeria is especially adapted to persons suffering from phthisis, rheumatism, scrofula, gout; also for lymphatic temperaments and old people; whilst it is equally disadvantageous to sanguine temperaments, corpulent persons, and all those who suffer from nervous affections, irritability, dysentery, hypertrophy of the heart or larger vessels.* In the case of consumptive patients, an early remove to the Algerian climate cannot be too strongly insisted on. They have then everything to hope, but in no cases should the invalid be sent out alone. Good English doctors and nurses are rarely to be heard of in Algiers; moreover, the simple sense of isolation militates against recovery.

It is perfectly easy to get excellent accommodation, good and varied food to please the

---

* "It is admitted by almost all French physicians who know the Algerian climate, that a residence in Algeria can ameliorate and even cure consumptive patients; twenty-one years' sojourn and medical practice convince me that this colony affords means of amelioration and cure."—DR. BODICHON, 1838.

daintiest appetite, and first-rate medicines made up from prescriptions.

But in case of a relapse or any unforeseen occurrence, I feel quite sure that a person in fragile health is seldom likely to rally unless soothed by the comforting presence of a relative or friend.

The Sisters of Mercy are good nurses in their way, but then they leave their patients at any hour of the day to go to mass, and worry him with all sorts of mummeries rather than omit a paternoster or sign of the cross.

Food is so important to the dainty and delicate, that it is worth while to consider what advantages Algeria offers with regard to meat and drink. The lover of game, fresh fruit and vegetables, will fare sumptuously every day; but the orthodox English taste for roast beef and mutton will be doomed to disappointment.

Whilst every kind of game and poultry is to be had all through the winter, with the adjuncts of green peas, fresh salads, and new potatoes, it must be confessed that meat is rather inferior to the quality we get in England.

Hotel accommodation is very good and moderate, and there are hundreds of pretty villas in the suburb, with all kinds of conveniences to be had. Nothing is easier than to establish oneself in one of these country retreats, and though one's French maids and Arab errand-boys do not at once fall into your way of living, all comes right in time.

And then how pleasant to get up early in the morning and go to the Arab market, your little Hamet or Ali following you, carrying two large baskets made of palm-fibre, which you fill as you go along! The market-place is all astir, although only seven o'clock.

Here is a flower-stall kept by a beautiful, melancholy-looking Moorish lad, who entices you into purchasing a bouquet of violets and roses as large as a soup-bowl. Then you come to a white-haired old Negro sitting on a doorstep making the prettiest baskets of *sperterin*, and strips of blue and scarlet cloth. Or you find yourself in the heart of fruit and vegetable stalls, piles of Blidah oranges and fresh bananas here, heaps of radishes and cauliflowers there, whilst wild-looking Arabs carrying fowls in their hands, push themselves in the way and screech out the cheapness of their goods, good-tempered Negresses offer you *galettes* on every side, you are glad when your little Arab's baskets are full at last and you can get out of the way.

It may be useful to say something about the summer, for though, as a rule, tourists return to England with the swallows, a few always choose to stay behind.

Is the heat of an Algerian summer indeed unbearable? Let us hear the reports of those who have experienced it. A friend of mine reports thus of the summer of 1865 :—

" Of course it was very hot, but I never felt so well in my life. My appetite was enormous, and I could sleep very well. For some days the sirocco blew, and then it was awful, even up here at Mustapha. The lovely prospect of the city, green hills, sea, and mountains, were all one yellow blur. If you touched a stone lying in the sun the skin came off your fingers. Dogs died of heat in the streets, and sun-strokes were of daily occurrence. The house was then full of Kabyle workmen, and they all took a siesta in the middle of the day, dropping asleep in the corridors—on the stairs

—just anywhere. It the evening it was pleasant, always except whilst the sirocco lasted."

A French author gives the following account of his experiences:—

" The rains have ceased. A drop of water
would be a phenomenon. The heavens seem
turned into copper. Nevertheless, the temperature maintains itself at moderate degrees.
I have seen evenings sufficiently fresh as to
make woollen clothes necessary. And from
mid-day till six o'clock we have the sea-breeze,
which produces the effect of an immense fan
and neutralizes the effect of the heat.

"I must now as a conscientious narrator
tell you something about the sirocco. It
was during the summer of 1860 I was turning over the pages of a book at the reading-
rooms, when the sun being too hot, I rose to
open the Venetian blind. As I did so I
felt myself repulsed as if by the flames of a
great fire.

" ' The sirocco!' cried some one close by.

" You have doubtless passed before the mouth
of a furnace or the brasier of a locomotive.
The sirocco produces precisely the same impression. The air was full of a dust so thick

and fine that one mistook it for a fog. One
perceived nothing of the green hills of Mustapha. The azure peaks of the Atlas were
drowned in a bath of fire.

" The passages, galleries, and arches of the
old and new town preserved their usual temperature, but in the broad open streets, and
especially along the quays, the heat was stupe-
fying.

" People put their hands in their pockets
and put up their coat-collars to protect themselves from the heat. The Arabs, whose
costume is so appropriate to the climate,
envelope themselves in their burnouses as
in winter.

" The leaves of the trees faded before the
eye. After minutes of a heavy and suffo-
cating calm, succeeded squalls of stinging wind.
The clouds of flying sand soon eclipsed the
obscured disk of the sun; and the different
shades of yellow, orange, saffron, and lemon
colour melted into a mass of copperish colour
impossible to describe. The covers of my
books were shrivelled as if they had been lying
a whole day before a fire. When in company
with some officers, I happened to touch the

sword of one of them, my hand was seared as if by a hot iron."

It is comforting to learn that this sirocco was considered quite exceptional; especially as this awful wind is a moral as well as physical poison. After a sirocco, there are always more quarrels, murders, and suicides,—a fact attributed to the irritating effects of it upon the nerves. Curiously enough, the fig-harvests are said to have the same effect upon the Kabyles.

During this season, the quantity of figs eaten is enormous, and a sort of intoxication follows, which formerly found vent in outbreaks against the French. There are so many causes and manners of excitement.

Germans say that drinking tea makes them talk scandal of their neighbours. The Norwich Brethren grew refractory over rusks!

But a word or two more about the climate of an Algerian summer. The great point to be insisted upon is hygiene. People should fall into the habit of taking a siesta; should take regular exercise morning or evening; should drink Moorish coffee; and, in fine, adapt themselves to the circumstances in which they are placed; imitate the Arab, and you can hardly do wrong.*

Twelve years ago an enthusiastic Algerian prophesied for his adopted country the most brilliant future.

In progress of time, he said, Algeria would become a privileged country, whither all the wealthy of Europe, possessors of country-houses and villas, should flock. The prophecy is not yet fulfilled, but I can imagine no pleasanter result of wealth than a Moorish house on the green Sahel overlooking the shining mosques and the blue sea crowned by bluer hills; or the combined interests, duties, and pleasures of a life that would be half European, half Arab, and wholly new.

* I abstract from Mr. Morell's book on Algiers the following observations made near Algiers a few years back:—

Temperature.

	Degrees of Réaumur.		Degrees of Réaumur.
January . .	11·64	July . . .	24·03
February . .	12·63	August .	24·71
March . .	13·33	September .	22·87
April . . .	15·02	October .	20·27
May . .	19·07	November . .	16·64
June . .	21·95	December . .	12·86

So fair indeed did I find the city of Algiers, so warmly was I welcomed there, so many-coloured and happy were the days of my stay, that these African souvenirs have, perforce, a certain sadness in them now.

The colours never fade from these pictures of memory, but they seem very far off, and I know well that, were I to "winter with the swallows" again and again, Algeria would never be quite the same place to me. For true it is as Goethe says,—

> " Gleich mit jedem Regengusse,
>   Aendert sich Dein holdes Thal,
>   Ach! und in demselben Flusse,
>   Schwimmst Du nicht zum zweiten Mal.
>
>   Du nun selbst: Was felsenfeste,
>   Sich vor Dir hervorgethan,
>   Mauern siehst Du, siehst Paläste
>   Stets mit andern Augen an !"

APPENDIX.

FOR those who are intending to " winter with the swallows," I have thought it advisable to add a few practical hints as to expenses, route, &c.

The journey to Algiers by Paris and Marseilles occupies four days and nights if made expeditiously, and costs between twelve and fourteen pounds. Arrived at Algiers, the traveller will have the choice of a variety of hotels, most of them moderate in price and well managed.

The Hôtel d'Orient, facing the harbour, entices most of my country-people by its imposing appearance, but I would put in a good word first for the comfortable, quiet, old-fashioned Hôtel d'Europe, where invalids are sure to be well cared for, and people with moderate means are as solicitously waited upon as those who travel *en grand seigneur*.

Apartments and furnished villas are to be found in abundance outside the town; but provisions are naturally dearer there, as everything has to be fetched from the markets, and no absolute economy is effected by private housekeeping; though of course it is desirable to move into the country when the warm weather sets in, and I have often found the temperature of Algiers like that of a blazing July day, when on the heights of Mustapha every one was glad of a little fire.

But as French is the language of Algeria, there is no difficulty in dealing with Arab shopkeepers or servants, and it is quite easy for English families to live comfortably without having recourse to hotels.

With regard to wardrobe, it may be as well to say a few words. Flannel should be worn next the skin, even more persistently than in England, and light woollen clothes are better for both sexes, as black cloth is unwearable in warm weather, and silk becomes whitened by dust and shrivelled by rain.

Ladies and gentlemen should both provide themselves with a mountaineering suit of water-proof cloth and strong boots, but they must not forget a warm dress for the coldest days and a light one for warm ones.

Black bonnets or hats are highly injudicious. The brilliancy of the sun and the dazzling whiteness of all the buildings in Algiers are very trying to unprotected brain and eyes, and ophthalmia is sadly frequent among the natives. White hats, white veils, broad bands of white cotton worn round the crown of the hat, are much to be recommended, also white cotton umbrellas.

The winter climate of Algiers is very healthy for children,—especially delicate children,—and though I have never heard of any English schools, masters are good and plentiful. Facilities for acquiring the French language naturally offer themselves, as in a French town, and no child need go untaught for want of opportunities.

I have mentioned the cheapness of living at such towns as Blidah, and it might be worth while for enterprising people of small means to set up schools and boarding-houses there, or even in Algiers.

European letters are received regularly three times a-week.

Service, according to the Church of England, is performed in a little building on the quay twice every Sunday.

English books (Tauchnitz edition) are to be obtained at all the best booksellers' shops.

Clothing of every kind is to be had at moderate prices, except English manufactures, which are dear.

Tea costs seven or eight francs a pound, and is not good.

Every one should take water-proof clothes, and a patent india-rubber bath, which costs little here, and is of incalculable value on a journey.

Rich people who " winter with the swallows," should, before starting, take an inventory of their threadbare linen and carpeting; for in no corner of the world are such delicate needlework and such gorgeous embroidery to be had as in the *ateliers* of the little Mahometan girls.

Sofa cushions, chair-seats and backs, curtains, handkerchiefs, scarfs, dresses, and underclothing, are soon made to order, and will be sure to give satisfaction and delight; one can superintend one's own orders, too, which is always an interesting occupation, especially in Algiers.

Invalids should set out for a warm climate with the swallows in October; but pleasure-seekers, or busy people who have only a month or two's grace, would do well to choose the months of March and April for an Algerian trip. By that time the winter rains are over, the summer heats have not set in, and excursions into the Tell may be happily made. Tourists—especially tourists who carry their sketch-books with them—might return by way of Constantine and Spain, thus seeing the curious and beautiful remains of Telemcen. The Biskrian Desert may be visited in about three weeks, and is a journey quite practicable to ladies. But those who are only able to spend a few months in Algiers will find their time amply occupied without making these long journeys.

There is no English guide-book of Algeria, and I therefore subjoin a short summary and table of expenses.

The city itself requires no guide - book.

Everything of passing interest is to be discovered by the intelligent traveller himself, and its past history has left little of general interest. But the precious Arabic MSS. contained in the Library will perhaps tempt a solitary scholar; and the Museum, which is under the management of a lady, deserves a visit from all; and the beautiful mosques, koubbas, and public gardens, will naturally attract every eye.

The traveller may vary his sojourn in Algiers by the following easy and delightful excursions.

First Excursion.—To Fort Napoléon and back, occupying from three to six days. Choose a dry season, as the rivers are impassable after much rain. Make a bargain with your coachman two or three days beforehand, that a relay of horses may be sent on; and arrange your party so as not to have more than three persons in each carriage. The average cost of a carriage and pair of horses is one pound a day, which sum includes the board of coachman; but as the road to Fort Napoléon is very hard, it is usual to pay a certain sum for the

entire journey, and not by day. I formed one
of a party of three to Fort Napoléon, and we
spent about five pounds each, the trip occupying three or four days. A cheaper way is to
take the diligence to the half-way station of
Tiziouzou, and from thence ascend on mules.
But the diligence service is often performed
at night, and is naturally much more fatiguing.
By a private carriage you reach Tiziouzou in
seven or eight hours. The best *auberge*, though
bad is the best, is the little hotel that lies some
hundred yards off the roadside to the right of
the traveller as he drives into the village. I
forget the name, but I do not forget a certain
bed in the other hotel, terrible as that of
Procrustes, and avoided by all Algerians.

Starting with fresh horses from Tiziouzou
early the second day, you reach Fort Napoléon
at noon, and have plenty of time to see the
fine views from the fort and a Kabyle village
or two. I do not particularise hotels, as it is
a case of Hobson's choice; but the traveller
fares tolerably well, and the beds are scrupulously clean.

Those who are not tied by time would do

well to choose the cheaper route by diligence
and mules to Fort Napoléon and remain there
several days.

For sportsmen and lovers of exploring, there
is ample employment, whilst for artists and
those interested in primitive manners and customs, the objects of interest are numberless.

One day's excursion I would recommend
all hardy travellers to undertake. Within a
few hours' ride of Fort Napoléon is a large
Kabyle town called Aït-Shanen, where those
beautiful arms, and those curious vases and
cups, are made by Kabyle men and women.
You return to Algiers by the same way.

Second Excursion.—To Blidah. The rail
carries you to Blidah in two or three hours,
and it is worth while to stay there a few days,
arranging with your host for board at a certain
sum *per diem.* The cost of *pension* in Algiers
is about fifty shillings weekly for each person,
but it is considerably less in Blidah, owing to
the cheapness of provisions. The English pay
more than any one else, it is evident, for I
made the journey twice, the first time with
some German friends, the second with a party
of my own country people. I need hardly say

that the hotel bill of the last journey almost doubled that of the first.

From Blidah you can make numerous excursions, not to speak of the lovely walks and drives in the immediate neighbourhood. Blidah is a very healthy spot, and is especially agreeable in the latter part of the spring, when the sun of Algiers blazes in a cloudless sky.

A very agreeable excursion from Blidah is that to Medeah by way of the gorge of the Chiffa. You can go by diligence, or hire a private carriage; in either case the trip costing very little, and occupying only two days. The gorge of the Chiffa alone can be seen in a few hours, and is one of the most wild striking spots in all Algeria. Monkeys are to be seen in plenty on fine days; and whilst the fern-clothed crags remind you of Devonshire, the rugged grandeur of the mountain-pass, in some places, recalls the Austrian Tyrol.

Third Excursion.—From Blidah to Cherchell, and home to Algiers by way of Tipasa. The journey to Cherchell occupies a long day, but it may be agreeably broken at Marengo, a thriving little colony at the western extremity of the Metidja. I have already dwelt on the

interest and beauty of Cherchell, the Iol of the
Carthaginians, and the Cæsarea of the Romans.
Here is still to be seen the ruined circus
where St. Marcian was cast to wild beasts, and
St. Severin and his wife, St. Aquila, were
burned together.

Giving a day to Cherchell, the traveller has
choice of two routes. He can either return to
Blidah by way of Tipasa, or to Algiers by way
of Kolea, seeing the celebrated *Tomb of the
Christian*. With regard to this monument,
there are so many legends that I have only
space to mention the latest and likeliest one;
according to which, it was a family of Mauritanian kings who were buried here. Seen from
the plain the pyramidal " Tombeau de la Chré-
tienne" is striking enough, but I had no opportunity of going to Kolea.

Tipasa is interesting both for its Roman
remains and natural beauty, and should certainly be visited. The roads are generally
good, and it is very rarely that one fares badly
with regard to provisions. But as it is often
advisable to rise very early when making these
excursions, I would counsel every lady to carry
in her portmanteau a tiny *Etna* and a little

tea. By this means one can make oneself a cup of tea in five minutes, whereas the waiters are almost sure to disappoint you of the promised *café de bonne heure.*

Fourth Excursion.—To the Cedar Forest of Teniet-el-Haad.

This trip should not be made till April, unless the traveller delights in snow-storms, and is a hardy equestrian. After heavy rains the rivers become impassable, and in February or March people are often weather-bound at Teniet for days, which was my case, though my imprisonment at Teniet was delightful enough.

You make Blidah the starting-point, and from thence take the diligence or hire carriages to Milianah, in the latter case sending on relays. Blidah is about seven or eight hours' journey from Milianah, but the drive is too interesting to prove long. Travellers can visit on the way the mineral waters of Hammam-Rira, the *Aquæ Calidæ* of the Romans. I cannot speak of the accommodation for visitors, having never visited Hammam-Rira, but the valuable properties of its springs will without doubt turn this solitary spot into a Schwalbach or Gastein ere long. The saline waters are especially recommended for skin diseases, neuralgia, rheumatism, sprains; and the ferruginous, for diseases of the liver, chlorosis, poverty of blood, and debility induced by dysentery, diarrhœa, fever, &c.

Milianah is superbly situated, and might form an agreeable halting-place for some days. The traveller bound to the Cedar Forest will do well to hurry on if the weather be favourable. From Milianah it is necessary to hire carriages or a guide and horses, for the diligences do not go beyond. Riding is preferable, as the excellent military road on which you travel so pleasantly for the first hour or two is not yet completed to Teniet, and one gets terribly shaken in crossing the river-beds.

Resting a night at the little caravansary, of Anseur-el-Louzi, you reach Teniet-el-Haad next day early in the afternoon. There is only one hotel at Teniet, and that one dear and dirty.

From Teniet excursions can be made into the Little Desert, which abounds in jackals, hyænas, wild gazelles, and all sorts of game. Panthers, and even lions, still haunt the forests of Teniet, but they do not leave their coverts till dusk. It is therefore highly unadvisable to remain in the forest after sunset, and indeed guides will not allow you to do so. Fishing is also to be had.

From Teniet you can return to Europe by way of Tiaret, Maskara, Oran, and Spain, the sea voyage occupying about twelve hours; or to Algiers by way of Mostganem and the coast. In the former case, one can visit Telemcen, one of the most curious and beautiful Moorish cities in Algeria.

Another excursion which offers, perhaps, more novelty than any other is that to La'ronat in the Sahara.

You start from Medeah and find comfortable accommodation in caravansaries all the way. La'ronat is surrounded by forests of palms, and if its panegyrists have not erred, is a lovely oasis worth every one's while to see at any cost.

A French writer says of it: " The gardens which surround the oasis are of a delicious aspect. The most lively imagination could not conceive a more marvellous and more luxurious nature. Imagine an interminable colonnade of palm-trees, whose plumy tufts rise

T

twelve yards from the ground; below are massed vines, peach, and apricot trees, the fig and the quince; whilst lower still, glow borders of flowers and lesser fruit."

Having now given the reader some idea of Algerian travel, I will say a word or two about such objects of interest and pleasure as lie within the reach of those who are unwilling or unable to make long excursions.

The Flora of Algeria is unusually rich, and a flower-painter would find there a new and inexhaustible field. I have plucked in a morning's walk more specimens of wild flowers than I could count, and the gardens are gorgeous beyond description in May and June.

Ladies might also employ their time agreeably in learning Arab embroidery, which is quite an art, a beautiful art too, and which by bringing them into contact with young Mahometan girls, might do something towards improving their condition.

The young Moor mixes freely with Europeans, and becomes a cosmopolitan in mind and manners. Why should his sisters be cut off from the same privileges? It is quite certain that the evil, if curable at all, is to be cured by the unproselytizing influence of good women.

The conchologist will find an infinite variety of shells on the coast, especially if he rise early and follow his search persistently.

The collector of coins, jewels, and curiosities, had better not come to Algiers, as he will be tempted to ruin himself by purchasing all sorts of treasures. Numidian, Arab, and Roman coins, Moorish yataghans and scimitars thickly inlaid with jewels, caskets of pearl, looking-glasses with jewelled frames worth hundreds of pounds, rich carpets and spoils innumerable of many a smala, are here to be had *ad infinitum*, as well as relics and precious stones.

The lover of music might spend his time worse than in collecting and arranging such Arab melodies as are familiar with every ragged *gamin* of the streets. Some of these airs are quaint and pretty, and have been effectively transcribed by a resident in Algiers, M. Salvador Daniel.

Another occupation occurs to me as particularly pleasant and useful. There are some beautiful illuminated Arabic MSS. in the library

276 *A Winter with the Swallows.*

well worth copying; and here and there in the Moorish town, one may meet with the ragged possessor of a superb Koran illuminated in colours and gold. The fortunate discoverer of such a treasure will do well to close a bargain at once, as these illuminated Korans grow more scarce every day. What more curious or precious souvenir of Algiers than copies of such beautiful work?

Algiers offers every opportunity for studying Arabic. There are public courses every day, open to strangers, and excellent French and native masters. The best, and indeed only plan to acquire colloquial Arabic, is to keep a native servant, to attend the Courts of Assizes, the Cadis' sittings, the markets, and to lounge about the bazaars. By this means you soon acquire facility in expressing yourself, which is infinitely more useful on journeys than lessons in grammar and the Koran. Of course the spoken Arabic of Algeria differs from the classic as the *patois* of Suabia from the German of Goethe ; but one must learn both. The best grammars are those published in Algiers.

French money circulates throughout the country, and the French language is spoken in all towns and villages. Only in the Desert, therefore, in isolated country places, and in the society of women, is a knowledge of Arabic really necessary; though no one can really learn to know a Moor or Arab without it. Arab guides are perfectly to be trusted, and will be generally found civil and intelligent.

The best way to keep oneself *au courant* with all that goes on in the town, is to make the acquaintance of one or two merchants. Drop in now and then to buy a pair of slippers, an ostrich's egg, or some Kabyle pottery, and you are sure to hear of a Moorish wedding here, an Aïssaoua fête there; a Negro dance to-day, a Sacrifice to-morrow. Or, in the case of gentlemen, go to the cafés and barbers' shops, and make yourself agreeable. By this means you are sure to hear the news of the day and see something of Moorish life.

In conclusion, let no one come to Algiers with the desire and intention of living *à l'Anglaise.* It would be dangerous if it were not impossible. An Arab transported to London at Christmas might as well dress himself in white cotton and try to live upon dates and *kous-kous*, as an Englishman wear black clothes and drink strong tea in Algeria. Climate is inexorable, and there is no alternative but to obey its laws.

NOTES.

 HAVE extracted some notes from an admirable little work, by Dr. Mitchell, on the climate of Algiers, with regard to pulmonary consumption, published in that city some years since and unknown here.

The site of Algiers is very nearly the same as that of many localities on the sea-coast of the Mediterranean, such as the south of Spain, Sicily, the coasts of Greece, and some places in Asia Minor. A little more northerly than Malta, Egypt, and Madeira, it approaches nearer to the equator than Nice, Florence, and Rome.

The Algerian year may, properly speaking, be divided into two seasons, the temperate and the hot. The mean temperature of Algiers resembles more nearly that of Malta, than that of any other place frequented by invalids. At Cairo, the mean temperature is higher by 1° 66′, and the winter colder by 2° 22′. The heat of summer is almost equal in Malta, Madeira, and Algiers, but the cold of the winter of Algiers more or less exceeds that of both places. The proportion of rain in the year is very nearly the same in Algiers as in Madeira, Malta, Gibraltar, and Nice ; but in these latter resorts of valetudinarians, the rain falls more equally during the different months. By comparing statistics, one finds that the days of rain number in London double what they do in Algiers, whilst in Algiers they very little exceed those of Madeira. Dr. Broussais describes the commencement of the year in Algiers as having a serene sky and a mild temperature. The clouds hide the sun from time to time for a few minutes, rarely for hours, more rarely still for days ; whilst the rain only falls for a short time, and not often in abundance; other writers speak after the same manner.

For myself, I have seen rain fall suddenly, obscuring the sky, flooding the streets, dispersing the passers-by, and rendering it quite impossible to remain out of doors. Hardly has the storm ceased, however, when the invalid can quit his room, and take exercise out of doors. The pavements dry up almost instantaneously, and the sun comes out. I firmly believe that an invalid wintering in Algiers would hardly be kept in-doors by the rain half a dozen days in succession throughout the six or seven months of his stay.

The predominating winds of Algiers are the north-westerly. South or south-easterly winds are rare. In this respect Algiers may be compared with Malta.

The climate may be regarded as dry and bracing. Dew is rarely seen during the winter and spring; it is much more frequent during the warm season, and in the valleys is found all the year round.

The sky of North Africa rivals, if it do not surpass, that of Italy. There is a beneficent influence in a limpid atmosphere and cloudless sky that we hardly value enough. For light indeed acts upon the functions of the animal system much more than is generally imagined.

The foregoing remarks will have demonstrated the tropical characteristics of the Algerian climate,— limited oscillations of the barometrical column; little variation of the thermometer; periodical winds and rains; shortness of twilight; cloudless sky. These are, however, to be considered as approximations only, for the real character of the climate is temperate rather than tropical. One may say, that during winter and spring it rivals that of Madeira; possessing the same degree of warmth, and a more unvarying temperature, whilst it is drier and less relaxing.

There is no perfect climate, however, and those who should come to Algiers expecting a sky of never-changing serenity, will certainly be disappointed; bad weather will happen sometimes, as everywhere else, but taking all things together, statistics and experience engage me to affirm that, there are few climates superior, or equally advantageous to valetudinarians, requiring a 'more reviving and less foggy atmosphere than our own.

We now come to the especial consideration of phthisis, or pulmonary consumption. Dr. Broussais says, " This kind of disease is without doubt much less frequent in our African possessions than in France; and the difference is so great that it can but depend on character."

According to Dr. Catteloup, another authority, consumption is very rare among the inhabitants of Algiers. Europeans are seldom subject to it, the progress of the disease is retarded, and it is very far from being constantly fatal.

Doctor Bertherand, physician to the Military Hospital of Algiers, makes the following statement :—" A sojourn of five years in the military hospitals, camps and towns of Algeria, have originated and strengthened these opinions. Phthisis is very rare in Algeria. The Algerian climate stops, or at least modifies, the progress of the formation of tubercles. According to my notes and recollections, the total figure of pulmonary affections treated by me during five years did not exceed fifteen ; of these, twelve were affected before the emigration ; five have died, and ten survive."

Dr. Foley, another practical authority, declares lung disease to be very rare in Algeria, both among Europeans and natives, and that the disease, if the patient be brought out here in an early stage, not only ceases to make progress, but shows a marked amelioration. Phthisis is altogether exceptional among the

Arabs, who call it *memdh-dhat*, the disease of weakness, and believe it to be contagious.

In conclusion, I may affirm that, firstly, statistics and the opinions of different physicians permit us to conclude that phthisis is a much rarer disease in Africa than in Europe or in North America.

Secondly. According to the same authorities, we may, upon sufficient evidence, presume other diseases of the respiratory organs to be also less frequent in Algeria.

Thirdly. The number and the class of witnesses to whom we have referred, lead us to believe that new researches will confirm these opinions more and more.

It is without doubt affirming much, when we declare that in Algiers, the formation of tubercles is arrested in those predisposed to it, and that in those already diseased, the progress of the malady is stopped, and the general symptoms so far improve, as to affect the appearance of a cure.

THE END.

www.ingramcontent.com/pod-product-compliance
Lightning Source LLC
Chambersburg PA
CBHW021038030726
47496CB00006B/1593